Thy Will Be Done

*Letting God Lead You Even When
The Destination Is Unknown*

A Novel By
SARAH VIDEGLA

KREATIVE WAYS

USA/AFRICA
Book 1 Of HIS WILL SERIES

Copyright © 2022 by Kreative Ways, LLC
Cover Copyright © 2022 By Kreative Ways, LLC

Kreative Ways supports the right to free expression and the value of copyright. The purpose of copyright is to encourage writers and artists to produce the works that enrich and empower our culture and more.

The scanning, uploading, and distribution of this without permission is a theft of the author's intellectual property. If you would like permissions to use material from the book (other than for review purposes), please contact kreativekids96@gmail.com.

Thank you for your support of the author's rights.
Kreative Ways, LLC
3415 Cottonwood Lane, Omaha NE 68134
July 2022
The publisher is not responsible for websites (or their content)
that are not owned by the publisher.
To stay connected to the author and all her upcoming materials and other works, visit:
www.sarahvidegla.com
www.thekreativeways.com

Library of Congress Control Number: 2022906885
ISBNS: 979-8-9857990-0-2 (paperback)
Thy Will Be Done: written by Sarah Videgla

~To Nouria, Samuel & Chloe-Grace,
Keep shining like the diamonds that you are~

You three are my miracles, blessings, and grace that's unending and I love you all so much…

Nadifa
Thanks for your love & support. May Allah Guide & protect you
S.V

Table of Contents

Prologue vii
One 9
Two 12
Three 15
Four 18
Five 21
Six 24
Seven 30
Eight 33
Nine 37
Ten 41
Eleven 46
Twelve 51
Thirteen 58
Fourteen 66
Fifteen 69
Sixteen 76
Seventeen 83
Eighteen 86
Nineteen 97
Twenty 104
Twenty One 110
Twenty Two 114
Twenty Three 121
Twenty Four 126
Twenty Five 130
Twenty Six 135
Twenty Seven 140
Twenty Eight 144
Twenty Nine 149
Thirty 157
Thirty One 164
Thirty Two 168
Thirty Three 173

Thirty Four	178
Thirty Five	184
Thirty Six	188
Thirty Seven	194
Epilogue	197
Acknowledgements	200
About the Author	202

Prologue

Looking out the window, she wondered what it would be like if she didn't accept his proposal. Would she still be traveling the world from one place to another and hoping for love to find her? Maybe, she would have settled down somewhere fun and tropical where she could enjoy the view of the ocean and its perks daily. Hearing a few footsteps, she turned around and saw Sophie beside her, holding an empty cup, and by her gesture, she could quickly tell that Sophie wanted water.

"Come on, Sophie, Mommy will get you your water."

Following her mother as if her life depended on it, Sophie was happy her mother understood her without saying a word. That had become a routine. Keyanna LeFevre had developed a keen understanding of her daughter ever since she learned that Sophie was autistic and had a speech delay disability. When she saw her daughter, Keyanna didn't care about autism. Instead, she only saw a beautiful and smart girl who could sing her lungs out. Grabbing the bottle of water, Keyanna filled up the cup and handed it over to a curious pair of eyes who was ready to run in another direction to play with her siblings.

Keyanna loved her children and was glad that on the verge of thirty, she experienced happiness daily from each of her amazing kids who were all unique: Sophie, Janis, and Elodie. Returning to her thoughts, she suddenly remembered that she was to meet her party planner, who was in charge of planning her thirtieth birthday. She quickly grabbed her purse and keys and headed out the door without forgetting to say goodbye to her children. Thank goodness for Kyara, a friend (turned sister) who had been a partner in crime since their high school days.

Today, Kyara agreed to watch the kids while Keyanna met with Joselyn, a party planner. Kyara had become a part of her, and Keyanna saw her as a sister she never had. They shared everything and knew each other's secrets like the back of their hands. More importantly, Kyara had stood with her during the hardest time of her life when her family didn't. Trying to stay focused on the road and forcing that thought of the past out of her mind, Keyanna blazed the volume of the radio and started singing her lungs out to DJ Kerozen's new song "Tu sera eleve." There was something about that song that she found herself drawn to at all times. The song had been on her playlist for the past several weeks, and she knew it would be there for years to come.

One

Sitting down in her chair, Keyanna glanced around and saw how beautiful the new Panera Bread Cafe looked. The decorations and setting were lovely and felt cozy. She was glad; the business had relocated to a more spacious building for this to happen. Panera Bread had always been one of her favorite spots for breakfast or lunch. Occasionally, she would bring the kids there for dinner on their "mommy's day out."

While getting up to get her drink, Keyanna accidentally bumped into someone.

"Oh, I'm so sorry. I wasn't paying attention to where I was going," she said out loud.

Trying to pick up the cup off the floor and straighten herself up, she came face to face with the stranger, who turned out to be an old friend.

"Eric, what are you doing here?"

"Well, I should ask you the same thing, Keyanna."

They immediately hugged each other and headed over to a table to sit down.

"I'm here to meet my party planner and grab lunch at the same time. When did you get back in town? How is your wife? And your father? Oh my, sorry, I'm rambling. You can see how excited I am to see you, Eric."

"Well, likewise. To answer all your questions, my dad is doing well and my now ex-wife is back in Atlanta."

Keyanna's facial expressions changed, yet she pretended as if all was well and decided to continue listening to him.

"I came back to town last night," said Eric. "And I will be here for two weeks before heading out to Uganda," he added.

"What in the world are you going to do in Uganda?" Keyanna asked.

"Well, you know me, I love traveling and providing care for people in need. I recently signed up for a mission trip through my church. They needed surgeons who can perform surgeries on women with health problems, deliver babies, and provide everyday care in remote places. I thought there was no better time than now to actually do those things."

"Yeah, I can see that," replied Keyanna. "I remember the happiness you had on your face when you were in the Peace Corps back in Angola during our college days."

"Those times were the best, Keyanna. I found my purpose there. Anyway, I have to run now. I'm also meeting a family friend here. Don't want to take much of your time."

"Don't be silly, and it was great catching up with you. Maybe, I could invite you to my birthday party next week. I will be turning thirty and thought I should do a little get-together for friends and family to celebrate."

"That's right, your birthday is next week. I remember it every year and since we lost touch, I never knew how to send you a gift or even a birthday card. I'll do my best to make time to stop by."

"Here's the invitation with my business card, as well. Call me, and please come by if you can. I would love to see you and continue our conversation from where we left off."

"Thanks, Keyanna, I'll call you to confirm."

Walking away, Eric couldn't help but to turn and see her from the back one more time. Coincidently, Keyanna did the same, and once their eyes locked, it felt as if they were communicating through them.

Uhhhh! How is it possible for me to still get all these tingling sensations when I see him? After all, it has been ten years since we both moved on with our lives.

Trying not to make anything out of it, Keyanna glanced down at her watch and wondered why Joselyn was not here yet. Just as she was getting ready to dial her number, Joselyn called out with a greeting.

Two

"Hi Joselyn, how are you? Did you forget about our meeting?"

"No, Keyanna, I wouldn't do that. I was caught up in a little bit of chaos this morning. I had a client who decided to cancel her wedding at the last minute. So sorry, I'm late."

"Oh, no worries. I understand completely. Things happen. Please have a seat and let me give you time to order your meal."

Once settled in and her order had been placed, Joselyn grabbed a pen and notebook to start the meeting.

"Before we jot down anything, I want to add one more guest to our guest list."

"Okay, who is that?"

"His name is Eric Johnson. He's an old friend from my high school and college days. I bumped into him and decided to invite him since we shared some of the same friends, and most of them will be at the party."

Now that she said it out loud, she wondered what Joselyn was thinking, inviting Eric of all people to her birthday party. This was not such a great idea. His presence alone, bringing all those memories back, could make things worse on that day.

Come on, Keyanna, aren't you exaggerating a bit? she asked herself.

Joselyn watched as Keyanna's facial expressions changed and waited a few minutes before calling her back to reality. Joselyn coughed a little to bring her attention back.

"I apologize, Joselyn, my mind somehow wandered for a minute."

"You think, lady. You took roughly ten minutes and even more during that day-dreaming session you just had. Okay, I was asking if Eric, the guest, would be bringing anybody."

"That's a good question. Well, he mentioned he just got divorced, so I'm not sure. He promised to call and confirm. Once I know, I'll get back to you with that."

"That'll be great! Now back to the planning. I have put down the deposit for the venue, scheduled the rentals, and am currently working with my team to bring your theme to life. Are we still keeping "African Queen" as the theme?"

"Of course, girl. I wouldn't change that for anything. Now even though African Queen is the theme, I don't want people to misinterpret it and run their imaginations wild as if the party would be like a jungle. The way people think sometimes when Africa is mentioned still baffles me, but we aren't letting that stop us from having fun and enjoying that day. I want something elegant yet simple. I was thinking of doing black and gold as the colors."

"That won't be a problem," answered Joselyn. "Black and gold will bring out the elegance and having only twenty-five people for the party will make it more intimate and close-knit. I'll have a final

PowerPoint of how things will be for you by the end of this week. Then we'll be ready for next week, and I know everything will turn out great."

"I trust it will, Joselyn."

"With that said, I have to run and will keep in touch with you throughout the week," Joselyn added.

"That'll be awesome. I can't wait," Keyanna smiled.

A few minutes later, Keyanna decided to head back home, too, because she had lost her appetite and didn't want to finish her meal anymore. She enjoyed her hot cocoa and knew that she would be full late into the day. Keyanna was never the type to consume too much and she was thankful for that. She recalled during her pregnancies how her metabolism changed and she gained so much weight before delivering each of her babies. Those were the only times she ate more than she ever did. She struggled to get back to her normal weight after each delivery and was glad now that she was done having kids. She could easily say that her beautiful shape was molding back to what it used to be during those college days. But it surely didn't happen overnight. It took a great deal of effort to maintain a routine of healthy eating and exercising to lose the weight.

Three

Dropping her keys on the counter, Keyanna shouted, "Is anyone home?"

No one answered. Usually, all three of her children would have run toward her for a hug. They were consistent at that and loved those times with her. Deciding to walk through the house, she moved from one room to the other with no signs of her kids. She then thought they went out on an errand with their Aunty Kyara. Keyanna headed down toward her bedroom, where she planned to dive into her bed and relax. Taking advantage of this little time for herself would be the best thing right now. Ever since she became a mother, having time for herself had become harder to find. And her support system had gotten better now that her parents moved back to Omaha, yet she still relied more heavily on her best friend than anyone else.

Once in a while, Keyanna hired a nanny so she and her husband could enjoy brunch or dinner, but it still didn't do justice to having a couple of days or weeks to themselves and enjoying each other's company. The past years had been hard on their marriage, and frankly, Keyanna didn't know if they could survive it. Lately, things had gone from bad to worse. Being a strong woman with faith with her only source of strength in God, she was still praying but felt as if prayers weren't enough. Pushing that thought out of her head, she changed her thinking and told herself that prayers were always enough. Experience had taught her that.

Turning the doorknob, Keyanna dropped her purse and fell glued to the ground. She couldn't move or talk for a few minutes. "Jesus, have mercy" were her next words. Then she yelled out the name of her husband. "Jules!" she shouted.

Shocked at hearing his name, Jules jumped out while knocking the woman on top of him down to the side. The woman struggled to find her balance and was doing everything to hide her face. She quickly gathered her clothes and ran out of the bedroom. Disturbed at what Keyanna just saw, Jules could barely speak a word out of his mouth. He stood there, pacing up and down, and wished the ground would open and swallow him alive. Keyanna managed to hold one side of the bedroom entrance wall and slide herself onto the floor so she would not lose her balance.

At first, it felt like a terrible nightmare and she wished waking up would erase all that she had just seen. A couple of minutes after gaining her strength back, she crawled into the room and to the side where her reading nook was and sat on a chair. Keyanna had always been an individual who never reacted when faced with the most hurtful experience. She was the type that kept everything inside. Some might say that's not a great way of coping with challenges and trials, but she coped well having that trait.

While finding her balance in the chair, Jules got up, ran out of the room, and went toward the guest room. He wondered what had gotten over him and how he ended up like this. Suddenly, feeling a load of shame, he decided to wash it off in the bathroom as if that would erase the scenario that he just created. Keyanna finally gained back the strength that she wanted to have, picked up her purse, and left the house.

Four

Getting into her car, Keyanna started driving with no final destination in mind. At the moment, she felt this would be some sort of therapy for her. Driving around town for hours, Keyanna found herself rejecting any calls that were coming in. She didn't even realize that she had driven so far away. Deciding finally to stop, take a break, and find a hotel to rest in, she suddenly realized that she had grabbed the wrong purse. This morning before heading out to meet Joselyn, she switched purses, and while getting back home after today's ugly incident, she must have mistakenly taken the empty purse.

"What kind of mess have I put myself into?" she mumbled out loud. Grabbing her cell phone, she dialed the number of the only person who could truly understand her.

"Hi, Kyara."

The next phrase she heard was from her friend. "Where are you, Keyanna? I tried to call you a couple of times but you seem to not take my calls.

Ignoring her best friend's question and trying to hide the pain in her voice, Keyanna rechecked to make sure that the children were safe with Kyara. She then proceeded to ask if her friend could send some money through a cash app. One thing Keyanna loved about Kyara was how she never questioned her whenever she asked for help.

"Are you okay, Keyanna? Your voice doesn't sound so good," Kyara asked.

Trying to play it off, Keyanna managed to say, "Girl, I'm fine." She went on to explain, "I ran out of the house to grab some Cold Stone ice cream but forgot that I didn't have my purse with me. I have my cash app card in the car, so I thought I could use that instead. So, will you please send me some money?"

Without hesitation, Kyara said, "Of course, love, I will do that right away."

Keyanna continued. "I came home but didn't see you and the kids. What are you guys up to?"

Kyara responded with a laugh. You know me, I brought them over to my place, and we are having a dance competition among the girls. The boys are busy playing games."

"Oh, that's great! Will it be possible to have them stay over for the night?" Keyanna asked.

"That shouldn't be any problem since you and I both took off this week to relax anyway."

"Thanks, Kyara! I want to use tonight to relax a bit and I'll pick them up tomorrow morning. Maybe you and I can have breakfast together in the morning before I take them home."

"Sounds good to me," replied Kyara. "Alfred is also home for the next two days, so he'll be happy to help babysit. I'll see you tomorrow at around nine or ten then. Alright? I've sent you the money through the app. You should receive a notification right about now."

"Yup, I got it. Thanks, you rock!"

Hanging up the phone, Keyanna realized how bad of a liar she was but thought it was the best thing to do for now. She would find a hotel where she could rest and think about what happened tonight. She also realized while looking at the cash app that she had money already in the account. She didn't have to ask for money and could have easily transferred money from her account to the card herself.

Shaking her head, she was somewhat accepting that this hit was deeper than she realized. While convincing herself of what was best, for now, she couldn't help but shed tears. But at that moment, she recalled her own affirmations: "I am the child of the Highest, His grace is enough for me, He has my back, He will never fail me, and above all, He is my strength."

Going into her Google Maps, Keyanna was able to find a hotel nearby. She drove over to the hotel and was going to get herself a room for the night. She planned to rest tonight and then head back to her children the next day. To her surprise, she not only went a far distance, but she had ended up in Kearney, Nebraska. Kearney was a small city that she visited with her children from time to time for the weekend. It's amazing how her spirit led her here. Despite all the emotions within her, Keyanna never believed there was a real danger. She wondered for a second if there was a message to all of this.

Five

Heading to the lobby of the hotel, Keyanna paid for her room and was given a key. As she rode the elevator to her room, she still pondered on how she managed to get this far out of town. This is a town where she had always felt at peace. She would always come here to reconnect and reenergize and, of course, play with her children. It is amazing how she came directly here when trouble hit without even planning it. Was that supposed to be a way God was speaking to her? She quickly pushed the thought to the back of her mind and used her key to open the room. While entering the room, she realized how beautiful the setting was. She never had been to this hotel before. Now, she saw the potential of using it again in the future. It was simple yet felt cozy and welcoming. It was nothing like her bed at home, but it would certainly do for the night.

Keyanna decided to take a shower and maybe grab something to eat. She somehow had managed not to eat anything else after that hot cocoa and now she could feel her stomach growling and calling out for food.

Stepping out of the hotel restaurant, Keyanna felt relieved and found herself enjoying the chicken noodle soup that the eatery made.

It felt like a homemade meal and this is one of the reasons why she loved this town. She headed to her room, after eating, and locked the door behind her. She was glad Kyara was able to come through with that money even though she had money on the card for it allowed her to buy some extra clothes and toiletries needed from the hotel shop downstairs. She was also glad that she kept a second ID in her car for emergency days.

Today was one of those days where she needed that ID and was glad this idea of hers paid off, after all. Laying in her bed, Keyanna found herself relieving the moment that had happened a few hours ago. *What was Jules thinking? Since when had he started cheating?* To top it off, she thought about their matrimonial bed. *How heartless could he be?*

Jules hadn't always been the greatest husband, but he was the greatest dad and that's one thing she appreciated about him. Jules had made sure he always provided for his children and cared for their needs. However, as a husband, he had work to do. To her, it seemed like he had become the opposite of what he used to be when they first met.

For Jules, showing affection and being romantic nowadays was a waste of time and money. She wondered how and what could have changed him so badly. He wasn't like that in the beginning. He was romantic and very affectionate; he catered to her needs and was a gentleman. However, year after year since they were married, it felt as if something switched inside him. He became this cold and uncaring person. He was always ready to give excuses for his wrongdoings.

He wouldn't go to church, would not pray, and tried as much to avoid time with her. He even refused counseling. How did he get so bad that now he had added cheating to the list? Keyanna had always seen herself as a faithful wife, no matter what the situation might be. Many occasions had presented themselves at the beginning of their relationship where she saw herself cheating, but she took the right course and didn't cheat. Finding herself crying again, she switched off her light by the nightstand and decided to just pray. It's amazing how prayer comes naturally to her now whether in a moment of pain or joy. Prayer over the years had become her peace when chaos was around or she felt it within her.

"Father, my Creator, my everything; you see it all, and you know it all. I am hurt, and I am confused about what's next, but you have a plan for me. Those plans are good, so I trust You and pray that your will be done. Be my strength, oh, Lord! Amen!"

Six

The sound of the ringtone made Keyanna jump. She switched the light on and stretched her arm to grab the phone. With her eyes half-closed, she didn't bother to check who it was.

"Hello!" The voice on the other side of the line was too familiar, and without thinking, she hung up.

"Why would he keep calling me?" she asked herself out loud. She wished he could stop calling and let her be. She tossed and turned for a minute and tried going back to sleep. The more she tried to get her sleep back, the harder it was. Turning the light back on, she eased out of bed, grabbed her robe, and headed downstairs. She looked down at her phone, after she got out of the elevator, and didn't notice that she was walking into someone. She quickly lifted her head to apologize and got the shock of her life.

"Eric? Are you stalking me or something? How is it possible for me to see you twice in one day?"

"You tell me," replied Eric. "What are you doing here in the middle of the night?"

"I should be asking you the same question," Keyanna answered.

"Fine, Keke, you won."

"Don't call me that," she demanded. "No one has ever called me that since our high school years. Besides, my first daughter goes by Keke now from time to time, so I want everyone to call me Keyanna instead."

"I'm sorry for calling you Keke. As for what I am doing here, I had a meeting with a colleague earlier today, here in Kearney, and decided to stay the night since it was late by the time we wrapped up."

"Oh, I see."

"What about you?" asked Eric.

"Well, it's a long story. But I usually come here to rekindle. I wasn't really asleep and was headed downstairs to get some ice cream."

"That's odd," replied Eric. "I was also going downstairs for the same reason. Do you still eat cookie dough?"

"Don't make it sound like you know me more than myself now, Eric. Yes, I still eat cookie dough, and it still is my favorite ice cream."

"Alright, why don't you head back to your room and I will go downstairs to get the ice cream? I forgot to ask, are you here alone?"

"Hmm, that depends."

"Keyanna, are you serious?"

"Yes, I am."

"Well, I was going to suggest we both sit down and talk while we enjoy the ice cream in your room if you are okay with the idea.

"That's fine. My room is 205, and I will wait for you there then."

A couple of minutes later, Keyanna was enjoying her ice cream while talking with Eric about their college days. They were a year apart in college. They also made sure they kept their relationship despite the pressure of their peers and college courses. He was majoring in pre-med while she was studying finance and economics with a focus on non-profit organizations.

Keyanna met Eric in her junior year when Eric transferred to Central Senior High from Atlanta. He was tall and handsome and walked with so much pizzazz that every girl wanted to be with him at the time. As a young girl, her focus was on graduating with a full-ride scholarship. Keyanna didn't care much then about what any guy stood for or their looks. Many guys had approached her at that time to date, but she refused everyone and told them that she wasn't ready to date. Her education was "her boyfriend" at the time. However, when Eric came along, all that changed. There was something about the way he approached her and how confident and humble he was despite his background. That attitude made her fall hard for him and consider his proposal.

They went on studying, playing, and doing almost everything together that year. Through those bonds, Keyanna truly learned more about Eric and how he wanted to find his purpose and not get sucked into the family business. Eric came from a lineage of business tycoons who owned a lot of agricultural land in his home country of Togo, West Africa. So, there were many expectations from his family for him after he graduated from college. However, Eric made sure they understood that the family business wasn't his purpose in life. This belief of having a purpose was so vital to him that he was willing to give up the family business and find his destiny.

That drive made Keyanna love him more, and with that, she gave her heart and soul to him. After graduation, Keyanna made sure to attend the same college Eric was attending. That dream came true when Keyanna joined Eric the following year at Delaware State University.

However, upon her arrival on campus, during the first weeks, Keyanna had realized that the Eric she fell in love with wasn't the same one she met on campus. Back then, she couldn't grasp what the problem was. So, she held her head high and kept the relationship going even if at times troubles emerged.

"Keyanna, are you with me?" Eric asked.

"What?" she replied.

"I asked if you would tell me the long story behind why you are in Kearney tonight?"

She took a deep breath and then spoke. "I found another woman sleeping with my husband in our bed."

There, she had said it out loud for the first time. And the first person who heard it was the one and only she had indeed given it all to in the past.

What was I saying? She loved Jules and cared for him. She did everything right by him.

But you know the love you have for Eric will always be different. She tried to ignore that voice and noticed Eric had stood up and wrapped her in his arms.

"I am so sorry, Keyanna. I wish there were more I could say, but that pain is hard and only prayer can help you with that."

She chuckled and asked, "What do you mean? You said that pain is hard to let go of, and only prayers can help. Have you experienced that pain?"

He held her tighter even more before releasing her and drew a deep sigh. "I didn't catch my ex-wife with another, but yes, I have experienced the pain. She came and opened up to me about her affair with another man. I didn't see it coming, so it took me on a roller coaster for months, and only heaven saw me through. I forgave her but just couldn't rekindle our marriage again, especially since she refused to have a child with me. There was nothing left to fix."

"I am so sorry, Eric. You mentioned earlier that you were divorced and given the fact that you and I haven't talked in years, I didn't want to pry into your business when you shared about your divorce. That's why I didn't ask anything else."

They both hugged for a long moment and all Keyanna could feel was how his scent still did wonders to her. *Why was I feeling all safe and okay in this man's arms after all these years?*

Little did she know that he was feeling the same way. Eric held on to Keyanna as if his life depended on it. *How long had it been since I hugged her? Hell, since she got this close to me.* He recalled how things ended back in college between them and wondered how she still talked with him as if it never happened. He hurt her deeply yet she forgave him and even communicated with him as nothing had happened. That quality was something he always admired about her. She had that quick forgiving heart that was hard for anyone to have. *God, I missed her so much! If only I could have the courage to say it.*

Deciding to end this long hug, Keyanna released Eric's arms and told him she was feeling sleepy and wanted to go to bed. There were barely three hours left until morning and she needed that sleep because tomorrow would be a long day. He acknowledged it and decided to stay and sit on the couch and watch over her.

"Oh no! You don't have to do that, Eric. I'll be fine. I'm not the young girl you met in high school who was afraid of the dark and would keep all the lights on before going to sleep. I've learned to cope and move on with that and I'm a full-grown woman now."

He nodded but replied, "I insist. I am not sleepy, so I can sit here on your couch while you sleep till morning."

"If you say so, feel free."

Seven

The sound of the water in the bathroom woke Keyanna up. She looked at the clock on the nightstand and realized she had entirely dozed off.

"Oh my, it's almost nine, and I am supposed to be at Kyara's place."

Keyanna got out of bed and headed to the bathroom. Forgetting that Eric stayed the night, she opened the door only to find him in the shower. She slowly tippy-toed and was backing out when Eric turned and said good morning.

"Good morning! Were you going somewhere?" he asked.

"I didn't mean to barge on you. I'll step out and wait my turn."

"No, it's okay. I'm just finishing, so come on in."

She hesitated a while, then took off her clothes and went in. At the sight of her, his countenance changed, and she noticed but acted as if all was good. She saw but pretended as if she didn't. Once in the shower, she turned her back to him and began to enjoy the feel of the water on her. Eric instantly grabbed her from the back and joined his lips to hers. He began kissing her as if he had just been given the go-ahead on forbidden land.

She responded with the same intensity. They were going at each other like two teenagers who had grasped the nature of kissing. Then slowly, Eric ended the kiss and walked out. She regained consciousness and shouted out loud a scream even the concierge downstairs wouldn't have missed.

She then came back to her senses and asked herself, *What was that? What just happened? How could I find herself sinning while running from one that her husband had committed?* She knew what just happened wasn't right but couldn't comprehend the whole thing. Trying to overthink it might result in more headaches so she released that thought for now. She quickly showered, dressed, and headed out of the motel. She still wondered what had given him the audacity to move in and shower in her room? He was supposed to only watch her sleep. She had created another entanglement in the midst of chaos. *I have messed up just like Jules*, she thought.

On the drive back home, Keyanna wondered how coincidental that was to meet Eric twice in one day. Then she recalled the kiss and how he had left when she returned from taking her shower. That was the typical Eric, always running away from problems. She recalled how he had also left her his last year in college, claiming he needed to find his purpose and needed time to do so. Some things would never change and she was mad for allowing herself to fall victim again to his seduction.

She knew he was a different person the moment she walked onto that campus but thought things would work out over time. However, she was wrong when he dropped that bomb back then. The worst part was how he did it. He didn't even dare tell her face to face. Instead, he left a note at the door. She spent that night crying and wondering what she did wrong. If not for her faith and how she had always depended on her Creator, she would have lost it. Now she had found herself kissing the same man after all these years. Almost ten years to be exact. Telling herself that there were more problems to be solved right now, she focused more on the road and noticed she only had twenty minutes more to get to her friend's house.

Eight

Upon arriving at Kyara's, she saw her best friend had made some omelets and French toast with strawberries for them to enjoy.

"When did you wake up to do all this?" Keyanna asked.

"Well, since you didn't call, I figured you were running late and decided it was best if I made something for us to eat at home," Kyara responded.

Kyara had always been a thoughtful person and Keyanna couldn't complain about that. She appreciated every bit of it.

"Thank you, best friend. I love you."

"I know," replied Kyara. "Now come on, let's dig in."

"Alright, but where are my kids and yours?"

"No worries, they went to the barbershop. My boys are due for a cut, so I asked Alfred to take all of them for now."

While eating, Kyara tried so much to keep to herself, but she couldn't do it. She knew Keyanna in and out and felt something was wrong. Based on the conversation that Alfred had last night with Jules, she was more than convinced that something had gone down.

"Okay, enough of the silent treatment, Keke. What's going on?"

"What do you mean?"

"Keyanna Marie LeFevre, tell me what happened between you and your husband."

Keyanna remained silent again for a while and then she spoke. "Why would you say that?"

"I know you and know something is wrong."

"Well, I caught Jules cheating with another woman in our bed."

"Holy Father. How could he do that? Oh, Keyanna, I'm so sorry. Why didn't you tell me all this while?

"I just found out yesterday, and up till now, I didn't know what to believe or even say."

Kyara got up, hugged her best friend, and held onto her for some time. She finally released her and sat down.

"Please tell me how it all happened."

Keyanna went on and told her best friend everything that happened as well as her meeting Eric.

.

Kyara took a huge deep breath and said, "I am very sorry for what happened to you, but through it all, you can't be transgressing while fleeing from one that was committed against you."

Dang it, she thought. She knew her best friend would say it the way it was. Kyara had always been an honest person and the Christian that she was made her blunter than any other person she had known.

Keyanna nodded in agreement and told her how Eric had disappeared again; it was the same way he did when they were in college.

Kyara let out a sigh of relief but reminded her best friend that it was up to her to confront her husband and have a talk with him. She went on to tell her how marriage was for better and for worse and, that with God, anything is possible.

"I am here to help you through this phase, no matter how hard it may be.

It was like yesterday when Alfred came home with another child and rocked my world. At that moment, everything was black in my head. I didn't even know how to go about it. All I wanted to do was to divorce Alfred. For not only had he cheated, but he also had a child out of our union. I was faced with the constant reminder of him being a cheater every time I saw that child, but I found my comfort and my sanity in the Bible."

Kyara continued speaking. "I am not saying it is easy, however, I'm asking you to try and find the root of all the problems and work on it together with God being in the middle. You will have to go back to those vows and submit them all under the cross."

Keyanna, with tears in her eyes, looked up at her best friend. She knew how hard it was for her Kyara at that time, and didn't truly understand how she was able to forgive him and take the child into their home. Today, that young child named Michael Yayra (Yayra Grace) was five years old. If not by his grace, their union would have ended.

"Kyara, you know I forgive easily, but I don't know how to cope with this situation."

"Then go to your Maker and let Him guide you. Only He can help you in this matter. As your friend, I will support you. But as your Maker, He knows you in and out and will direct your steps."

Nine

"In all your ways, acknowledge Him, and He will make your path straight."

That was the verse that came to mind when Keyanna parked in the driveway of her house. She genuinely wanted her marriage to still work out and was one who didn't believe in divorce.

Heck, her parents wouldn't have it any other way. She came from a family that held marriage very high and believed that God was always at the center. Anyone who truly understands and fights for it can make it. Her parents Rachel Dubois and Pierre LeFevre had proven that with their union lasting more than forty years now. Keyanna was their only child, and their expectations of her were very high. They felt betrayed and shocked when their daughter came home pregnant during her junior year in college.

Back then, Keyanna could vividly recall how their reactions were when she came home and announced her pregnancy as well as the ending of her relationship with Eric. Her parents were aware of her relationship with Eric, but they didn't know that they were sexually active. She recalled how her parents sat her down and told her that they would not be part of this journey. She was to find ways to cope until she gave birth to the child and also ways to raise the child while finishing her college degree.

At that time, Keyanna felt rejected and abandoned, but with prayers and the help of her best friend and her best friend's mother, she overcame it.

Kyara's mother, Eugenia Hopkins, lent her the helping hand she needed and had her move into their home to assist with the pregnancy and the birth of her child Sophie. Eugenia thought of Keyanna as her own and was a retired widow at the time; she felt she had more time on her hands for such a thing anyway. With her assistance, Keyanna coped with the pregnancy and delivered the baby at ease.

Getting back to her current dilemma, Keyanna stepped out of the car and felt glad the kids were still with her friend. On her way home, she called Jules and asked him to meet her at home so they could talk at length.

Upon entering her living room, she noticed the balloons and flowers that were on the table. The balloons had "I am sorry" written on them, and the flowers were huge. There were probably two dozen white roses. She appreciated the gesture, but this was the wrong time for romance. To think that she had wanted this romance for so long; now he was showing that trait. A voice reminded her: *Don't be bitter. Let the Spirit guide you in this conversation and meeting.*

With ease, Jules got up and fell on his knees. "My love, I know I have hurt you deeply and words can't fix it. But I am willing to try and make this union work and rewrite this terrible chapter of our lives."

She grabbed his hand and helped him up while heading to the sofa to take a seat. "Jules DeSouza, you are my husband, and I love you very much. But what you did will take some time for it to be alright. You know my stand when it comes to divorce, so that will not be an option."

There was more to be said. "However, prayer, counseling, and working on better communication will be the first step into rewriting the story as you said. While we are at it, I need you to know that I also kissed someone yesterday. I am not perfect and I know you aren't either. If I can sin, I can also understand how easy it might have come to you given our marriage hasn't been the best lately. The only thing I can't shake was why in our home? What if the children were here? What If I had walked in with my friends or my parents? For the sake of our children, I will still share our bed under the condition that you will get a new mattress, bed, and linens today. You will also go and get tested this week as well as in the next three months and six months again before you and I can talk about intimacy. I can't trust you when it comes to that area right now."

Keyanna had more suggestions. "I also would like for us to start couples' therapy with our pastor as soon as possible. Moreover, you will restart your journey with God and lean on Him so this marriage can work. I believe that your action yesterday is a result of a sequence of many things. The husband I have cannot betray me in that way. It's right that you can never know someone enough, but I know you, Jules. Despite the wrongs that you have done, I can still see that kind and loving soul that cherished and cared for my daughter and me almost ten years ago when I didn't have my family support. I cannot give up on you because you didn't give up on me."

Tears filled his eyes, and all he could say at that moment was thank you. "Thank you, Keyanna, for being a supporting and caring wife. Your heart of gold is like no other. I promise to do right by you from now on, and I accept all the terms you have laid down for us. I am genuinely grateful that you have decided to give us another chance."

Keyanna replied by saying, "I am not promising that there will be happy days and that the pain in my heart has disappeared because it hasn't. All I am saying is that I am willing to try if you will try as well. I am also apologizing for kissing another man. That was wrong of me and I pray you can forgive me, too.

Ten

Jules had kept his part of the promise and changed everything his wife had asked of him, as well as getting tested even though he swore he used protection. Keyanna rearranged the house to help herself feel at home and to welcome the journey she was embarking on with her husband. An entire week had passed by since the incident, and after one therapy session, she was keeping her hopes up. Jules had finally started praying again with her every morning and night. He was now the one who reminded the family about the morning prayer time.

Keyanna, on the other hand, continued to rely on Psalm 91 and Psalm 5 for daily devotions and asked God for strength and that His will be done in their lives.

Hearing the laughter throughout the house, she thought of how blessed she was with three beautiful children. They came with their challenges, but she wouldn't trade them for anything in the world. It seemed they were having fun dancing on that Nintendo Wii WWII video system with their father. She couldn't remember the last time music wasn't played in this house. Music was at the center of their everyday lives and Jules used it to bond with the children. Keyanna needed to get ready to go check out the venue for the final time. It was her birthday event tomorrow. She hadn't canceled it despite what she was going through in her own home. She wanted to have a great time with her friends and family. That would help her through all of this.

Later on, Keyanna entered the venue and was speechless. The place was simply breathtaking.

"Joselyn, you did an excellent job," she said.

"I am glad you like it," Joselyn said, smiling.

"Girl, no, I love it, and I think everyone will, too. It's like you were actually inside my head and could visualize it all. You have proven to me that you know your craft, and I am truly thankful. I can't believe tomorrow is the party."

"Yes, it is, and I am super excited. So, you still haven't heard from your old friend Eric on whether he can make it or not?" Joselyn asked.

Keyanna tried to ignore the question but knew she had to respond.

"I haven't heard back from him, Joselyn, and frankly, I think he won't make it," she finally answered.

The next day, the family was busy. Getting ready for the party, Keyanna had her best friend do her makeup and make sure she looked stunning. Being a girl that cared less about makeup and all those shenanigans, Kyara wanted to do her best, so Keyanna could appreciate it this time. Keyanna had always been the one who insisted on being natural and never used anything to enhance her beauty. Kyara, on the other hand, was the queen of it and was always happy when Keyanna asked for her help on days like this.

Finishing her last touch, Kyara stepped back for Keyanna to see her magic, and all Keyanna could say was "Wow, I love it! You are simply the best!"

Joselyn smiled. "I know it," she said. "Now, come on! Let's get you to your party."

Having her parents in town for the event, Keyanna made sure they would bring the children to the venue at the cake-cutting time so they could share that moment with her.

The crowd welcomed Keyanna with stunning applause when she entered the venue. She almost lost her balance but regained it with the help of her husband by her side. The wall's design, with a different print of patterns that African tribes used on their huts, gave the room a sense of a kingdom. The entrance had two men guarding it with their swords held in their hands. They all wore Ankara attire, so did the guests and Keyanna. The main table was centered with two other ones aligning parallel to it. They were all decorated with black and gold fabric while different colored handmade African baskets were arranged on top. Some baskets were filled with cowries that represented currencies in the Kingdom of Africa at one point. Others held kola nuts, a necessity for prayer in the old days, and even now while some also held a white eggplant, a fruit that is simply delicious and consumed daily by many Africans.

In the four corners of the room were handmade huts that had different prints on them. The servers dressed in uniforms made out of Ankara prints as well. Keyanna fell in love with everything and was happy she chose this particular theme. Being born in the United States to Nigerian and Togolese parents, her friends, at times, tended to forget her roots. She had always loved her roots and wanted to show this through the theme. Seeing all of the decorations helped her recall all the trips she took with her parents most summers when they went to Nigeria, Togo, or the neighboring countries. Africa is a beautiful continent, and she sometimes wished that people would explore it more.

Sitting down at her table, Keyanna felt loved because she had the right people sitting next to her: Jules, Kyara, and Kyara's husband, Alfred. And her friends, colleagues, and some family members were also at the event. Today was her day, and despite the pain in her heart, she wanted to enjoy this dinner party and her entourage. Joselyn came and reminded Keyanna of her entry speech and gave her a microphone. With the microphone in her hand, Keyanna stood up elegantly and began to speak. Her first words were "Mia we zon" which she translated as "You all are welcome," telling the crowd that was her mother's language "Ewe" from the people of Togo, West Africa.

Keyanna continued speaking by acknowledging everyone and saying how grateful she was that everybody could come.

"Now, let's say a prayer before the food is served," she said.

Jules stood up boldly and said, "I will do that for you, my love."

He then proceeded by saying, "Father Almighty, we thank you for this day and the many blessings you have showered on to us. As we gather here today, we pray for peace, your divine protection, and we bless Your name for adding another year to my wife's life. Continue to guide and protect Keyanna and guide her toward her purpose and all You have written for her life. Bless this meal and in Christ our Savior's name, we pray."

All joined in with a big "Amen."

After the prayer, everyone enjoyed the delicious dishes that were on the menu. The menu consisted of simple hors d'oeuvres of samosas and meat pies. The next course was African salad, also known as "Abacha" in the Igbo language. Finally, the main course was pounded yam, fufu, and lamb meat porridge. With no hesitation, Keyanna enjoyed the food while using her hand to show how the natives eat back home.

The evening went on as planned, and the personnel for the party was on point. Finally, the time for the cake arrived. So did Keyanna's children with her parents. Upon entering the hallway, her parents thought the place was stunning, and they felt proud of their daughter for creating this beautiful theme. Keyanna welcomed her parents and they all walked to the cake stand for the birthday wish. The crowd sang the *Happy Birthday* song to the birthday lady, and at the moment when she was ready to cut the cake, the unimaginable happened.

Eleven

"Mommy, look stranger!" Those were Sophie's words when she saw the gentleman walking into the venue. Everyone's attention was on the stranger that Sophie was pointing to. Most of them knew the stranger wasn't really a stranger, after all. It was Eric! Walking in a handmade Ankara suit with a hint of the colors of the theme showed how well he was built. His broad shoulders and well-designed facial features also showed how masculine and handsome he was. He also knew it and took in all the attention he was getting.

Keyanna almost dropped to her knees but fell back while her best friend caught her. The only thing that was running in her head was what if people saw the resemblance between him and Sophie. No one except her parents, Eric's parents, her husband, and best friend knew that Eric was Sophie's biological father. People in town had made the connection but dared never to ask. Many questions ran through her mind. *Why was he here?* He never confirmed the invitation; that's why she was comfortable for the children to come and celebrate with her. Keyanna felt her world crashing in on her at that moment. However, with the help of Jules, who grabbed the microphone and regained everyone's attention, the party continued and the cutting of the cake followed.

After enjoying the dessert, the guests mingled with each other and enjoyed the décor. Eric used that opportunity to get closer to Keyanna and her children. He had to admit that even though Keyanna stated that Sophie and Janis were autistic, he couldn't see any difference between them and other children. They were fun and had a lot of energy like children their age. One thing he couldn't get out of his mind was how Sophie looked like his own mother. He could have sworn that she even took her mother's nose. Maybe it was the alcohol messing with his head. Trying not to let that bother him, he apologized to Keyanna for not confirming his invitation and also leaving without a word the last time they saw each other. All she wanted at the moment was for the party to be over so that she could go home with her husband and children. She didn't want Jules to know it was Eric she had just kissed a few days ago.

Being in the same room with Jules and Eric was difficult for her emotions and she didn't know how to cope with it. Kyara saw this and did her best to stay close to Keyanna and help keep her nerves calm. Keyanna was grateful for Kyara. But she thought it was time to wrap up the party. She asked her husband to announce that they were retiring for the night, but everyone was welcome to say and groove until midnight. The servers and other personnel would be available until then before they needed to clean up and have the guests leave.

While heading out, Keyanna took the time to thank Joselyn for the great work she did. Then Keyanna put her in charge of all the gifts and asked her to have them brought to her home the following day. Joselyn said this wasn't a problem and she would do as Keyanna asked. Jules made sure his family got into the car safely and drove off to their home.

Keyanna was shocked at what she saw when they got home. There was a trail of lilies that kept going from the entrance of the house to her bedroom. She followed the flowers with a surprising look, while Jules went toward the children's rooms to help them clean up and get into bed. Rushing to see what was in her bedroom, Keyanna found herself hitting her toes on the corner of the door. She finally opened the door and stood there, amazed. The trail of lilies led to more lilies on her bed. The flowers were placed to write the words "I am sorry" and "Happy Birthday." She felt overwhelmed and happy and couldn't contain the excitement so she screamed and fell on the bed. A part of her thought that she had her man back while the other part told her that she was in too much of a hurry and there was still work to be done.

Even though Keyanna knew there was still a lot of work to do on her marriage, she couldn't help feeling that better days were ahead. She knew this storm would surely pass just like many have done before.

Deciding to take a shower before retiring to bed, Keyanna stepped into her bathroom and found more surprises. The entire bathroom floor was also filled with white and red roses. The bathtub had plastic candles lit around it, and there was a bottle of champagne with two glasses on a small cart near the tub. There was also a small box with a card on top of it. She couldn't help but cry. She missed this part of her husband and was glad he was working toward becoming better. She quickly took the card and opened it up. There was one sentence, "I will make it up to you every day of my life."

"What a pleasant surprise," she murmured.

The wrapped box that accompanied the letter contained a beautiful white gold necklace that was engraved with the words: "Forgiveness. Grace. Love."

Keyanna took the time to thank her husband for the beautiful surprise as well for him being there for her throughout the party when she got into bed after her bath.

A couple of hours later, she found herself still wide-awake thinking of the night she just had and all the tasks ahead of her. Marriage sure was difficult when you thought about the challenges that it brought. She was ready for whatever may come, for she could do anything through Christ that strengthens her. Saying a prayer, Keyanna dozed off and only got up when she felt the presence of someone in front of her. Opening her eyes slowly, she already knew who that was.

Sophie had the habit of coming into her parents' room since she was two years old and staring at her mother while she was asleep. Over the years, Keyanna had gotten used to that and sometimes looked forward to it as her wake-up call. She opened up her arms as Sophie snuggled in her bed next to her. *Can love be anything more than this?* she asked herself. Keyanna wouldn't trade that for anything in this world. Eric surely didn't know what he was missing.

Deciding not to bother herself with such negative thoughts this morning, Keyanna snuggled back under the sheet with her angel next to her. Sophie's warmth felt good and she praised God for helping her keep this child.

This was one of the reasons why she could never quit her marriage without giving her best to make it work.

An hour or two went by again before Keyanna arose from bed and made breakfast for her family. For once in a long time, the family sat at the table together, said a prayer, and enjoyed their meal. The kids were very happy and loved the strawberries topping their homemade buttermilk waffles. Keyanna loved making those for them; it was one of her favorite dishes for breakfast. Breakfast went well and, afterward, Jules and Keyanna told the children how they would be going on a trip next week. They explained that Mommy and Daddy needed a vacation to reconnect and how the children would also be enjoying a week with Grandma and Grandpa by doing all the wonderful things they love doing with their grandparents. The kids were very happy and wished for next week to come right now.

"Do you remember what today is?" Jules asked the kids.

They all shouted and said, "Family Fun Day!"

"Well then, let's get ready!" Jules told them.

Family Fun Day was a day to rest and spend time with the children. Keyanna and Jules planned to visit the Children's Museum and do some activities with the kids. They loved that place and Keyanna couldn't wait to see the smile on their faces when they got there.

Twelve

As imagined, the kids were so happy when they arrived at the museum. There were new exhibits to explore and different activities to sign up for. For the fear of missing it all, they couldn't choose their first program. Jules, being the great father that he had always been, stepped in and helped them decide. They then made a list in their heads of what would follow and made sure their dad held them accountable for it in case they mixed it up.

After that, the remainder of the visit went by so fast. Jules, Keyanna, and the kids explored the Science Center, aquarium, and, of course, the Imagination Playground. The girls also discovered America in Zanzibar and Fairytale Land. While heading out, they got a chance to buy some souvenirs from the museum shop.

Looking at her children and husband, Keyanna said a little prayer of thanksgiving to her Maker for a blessed and amazing day with her family. The Omaha Children's Museum had always been a great place for her children, and she was glad they once more created a memory that would last a lifetime for them. Her family was so important to her and she was determined to rebuild this foundation that seemed to have gotten some bruises along the way. When Eric left her, she never once thought about having such a thing as a family one day but the good Lord in his infinite mercy made it possible for her.

A couple of hours later, the family reached their home. After bathing the children and feeding them dinner, the family retired to a *Frozen II* movie which bought the non-stop singing of the girls and the repetition of Olaf's words for Janis. Sophie had learned to sing before she talked; it was a gift Keyanna believed came from God. Keyanna had spent her entire pregnancy asking God to bless her child with the gift of singing so she could sing for Him and also protect her and guide her. So, when Sophie was a toddler and couldn't speak but sang, Keyanna knew God was working through her. Despite all of that, she found the courage to seek answers to what was going on with her child. Sophie had delays in every milestone of her early years. Being a first-time mom made it difficult because she didn't know what to expect. She read books upon books and, finally, *The Autistic Brain* by Dr. Temple Grandin helped her understand some of the symptoms that Sophie was experiencing. With that, she and Jules started making inquiries, and not long after, their baby girl was diagnosed with autism by the age of three. They then went on to learn more about autism and how each case was different. She was thankful for all that they had learned over the years but, still, she knew that everything would work for the good of her child. Today, Sophie is overcoming all those barriers, speaking more, and understanding what has been taught to her. Keyanna could only thank Yahweh for His amazing grace placed upon her.

Keyanna often thanked Yahweh with these words: "Let your

light continue to shine upon her, Janis, and Elodie as well."

Once the movie came to an end, the children performed their bedtime routine and went to bed. As always, a family prayer was said and goodnight kisses were shared. Keyanna longed for her husband but reminded herself of the process that was put in place and how crucial she wanted to follow it. They were still sharing their matrimonial bed, a bed Jules had changed upon her request, but she would not be intimate with him again until the six-month time frame that she had given him for testing. After all, they have just started counseling and she wanted to try counseling for a longer period of time before anything else.

With that said, she simply kissed her husband goodnight and went straight to sleep.

Jules thought to himself: *How have I been so blind to all of this? How did I end up here, Lord? Please forgive me and help me rebuild this trust that I have broken. I love her and surely don't want to lose her.* Those were his prayers for his family that night. The guilt and shame were eating away at Jules's heart but he was determined to overcome them. He found himself praying short prayers throughout the day for strength and peace and, most of all, for the forgiveness of his sins. He couldn't imagine a life without his wife and his children. They were a part of him and he was a part of them. He wanted to overcome this temptation that almost destroyed him and what he held so dear.

The next couple of days, things were smooth within their household and it was time for everyone to pack and leave for their retreat.

Somehow, Keyanna felt some kind of anxiety and fear. As humans, we all fall into fear at times; but strength and knowing that God is there makes it easier and helps us relieve all those negative energies. So she decided to follow through with the plans and hope that this trip would indeed help them build a new foundation.

On their way to the airport, they made a stop at her parents' house where the kids were dropped off to spend a week. The children were excited about the amazing time they were going to have with their grandparents. Keyanna's parents had always spoiled them rotten as any grandparent would. Keyanna didn't always agree with her parents' parenting style. But for a couple of days, she had learned to let it slide to keep the peace. Sophie, Janis, and Elodie gave their parents huge hugs and kisses and rushed through the front door of their grandparents' house as if they were at the entry of Disney World and couldn't wait to start exploring the kingdoms that existed.

Jules thanked his in-laws, then backed up the truck to the main road that led them back to the airport. The destination was Freedom, Maine, a place both Jules and Keyanna had never visited. This was a suggestion by their pastor. He recommended it as one of the top ten best destinations for couples to reconnect and rekindle. For him, if they couldn't find themselves here, then they would never find themselves again for he truly believed that they would encounter God in this open place filled with His amazing handiwork.

The Couple's Nest was located in the city of Freedom, Maine. Keyanna had researched a little bit to know more about Maine, in general. She learned that it was a very small city with nearly a thousand people. One thing that did catch her attention was the famous restaurant called "The Lost Kitchen." This was a place she dreamed of visiting at one point in her life because of the good things she heard about it and the show that had been on the Magnolia Network Channel recently about the restaurant. The restaurant only takes reservations via mail if you want to reserve a spot. That's because the restaurant is open only six months of the year. Keyanna had always been a fan of things that were unique and different and this was one of them.

 The flight from Omaha, Nebraska to Freedom, Maine was a bit complicated. It consisted of a two-three hour flight with a stop in Charlotte, North Carolina before arriving at Bangor International Airport, Maine. Then from there, the couple would have to rent a car and drive for an hour before reaching their destination in Freedom. For Jules, it was a perfect scenario for both of them to talk and to think through all that had happened these past years and the reason why they were heading out on this trip in the first place.

 As far as Jules could remember, Keyanna and he hadn't had a couple's retreat trip in a while. When he got together with Keyanna, she was already pregnant with their first daughter but it was only one child so that never stopped them from exploring the world. Their first trip was to Montreal, Quebec and they enjoyed every bit of it. Keyanna had some friends there and that helped them explore the city and the surrounding area. Those were good times he recalled as his mind drifted back to focusing on the road to the airport.

Soon, they arrived. It's a good thing they left early because the airport was packed. Jules parked the car in the long-stay garage. Then, they got their bags and headed out to the check-in counters to get their tickets.

To make the trip enjoyable for them, Jules's father gave them first-class roundtrip tickets. While confessing to his sins, Jules shared those details with his dad who prayed with him throughout the couple's therapy sessions these past eight months. Jules's father was actually proud of his son for putting such an effort into his marriage after he thought he was on the verge of destroying it.

The couple finally got their boarding passes and was waiting for their flight. Boarding would soon start. Keyanna took those few minutes to get water, some candies, and a magazine that she could skim through during the flight. The flight was two hours non-stop to Charlotte. She didn't know how the trip would be since the couple had not talked much since the ride and the check-in process. Nevertheless, she would try to converse with her husband so a better atmosphere could be created before they arrived at their destination (the Couple's Nest).

Tired of the silence, she asked her husband how he was feeling about the trip. Jules looked at his wife with love, a love she could swear she hadn't seen for a long time.

Then, he answered, "I am hopeful and trusting God to help us through this process. I am all for 'Trusting the process" as we say all the time."

Keyanna grinned and replied, "For sure, I have asked God for

His will to be done for us in this marriage so I am trusting Him as well."

An announcement was made that it was time to board. Jules gathered his wife's handbag and his backpack, reached out to help Keyanna stand, and held onto her hand while they walked to the door leading to the plane.

Thirteen

Keyanna was not expecting such nice weather in Maine, but she would cherish it before she went back to Omaha. According to her research, the month of April should still be cold in Maine, but she noticed it was much nicer than what the weather was like currently in Omaha. Keyanna and Jules had packed for whatever the weather might be like so she was glad for that. The couple jumped into their super shuttle which led them to Freedom and their destination. Both of their flights had gone smoothly and they were just happy to be on the ground now.

Being the only two in the shuttle, Jules scooched over to be closer to his wife. He rested his head on her shoulder and started to fall asleep. Seeing that he dozed off, Keyanna shifted her body in a better position to accommodate his head so he could be comfortable. Looking at him made her remember all the reasons why she married him. He was a caring, passionate person who would go to the moon and back for anyone he cared about. She just couldn't comprehend how they ended up where they were now. Something broke within her husband and maybe inside her, too, and she wanted to make sure they fixed whatever it was.

It was a great afternoon, sitting in the park with her firstborn in her stroller and thinking of her life when she saw Jules doing laps around the field in the park. They had been friends for almost two years now and he hadn't been pushy at all or asked her to date. He had been very patient and just helped her. Today, somehow, she saw him from another perspective. Something was different. Watching him run and taking small breaks and seeing his body sculpture awakened some feelings in her that day. After all, it has been closer to two years since she had been intimate with anyone. From finding out about her pregnancy to giving birth, Keyanna was too hurt to contemplate anything sexual with another person and her faith wouldn't allow her to think otherwise.

During that time, she knew she had never gotten over Eric and couldn't imagine another man touching her. It was Eric or no one else. But at this moment, Jules got her attention. She was glued to watching him and, at some point, forgot that Sophie was in the stroller. She couldn't even recall how long she was fixated on him; the only thing she remembered was him standing in front of her and letting her know that Sophie was crying. She twitched and came back to herself and noticed that she was daydreaming about a man, and that man was right in front of her. She quickly apologized, then greeted him and picked up her child to calm her. It was then and there that their relationship began in her heart. She felt more for him and was ready to finally give him a chance. She would go to the park more than usual and see him working out there on most of the days. She started to give him more attention than she ever did before. For the past two years, Jules was in her life as a friend but this time around, it was more than that. She could feel it and so could he.

At first, Keyanna wouldn't embrace the idea but thank God for being best friends. Kyara was the one to motivate her to go and give dating a try. She reminded Keyanna how she couldn't stay single forever and wait on someone who didn't even know she existed. With encouragement from her best friend (and her best friend's mother), she gave it a try and that relationship became the marriage she had now. She and Jules dated for a year before tying the knot.

It wasn't easy when it was time to marry because she wasn't speaking to her parents at that period in her life. She felt very disappointed at them for rejecting her and her child. She realized that getting pregnant in college wasn't the ideal thing, but her parents washing their hands of it was the worst thing any parent could have done to a child who was in distress. She prayed that she wouldn't do that to her children. Jules had been a very supportive person those days. He encouraged her to forgive them and use the Bible as a reference in all these reassurances. It was him who taught her the importance of forgiveness and how to forgive someone meant freeing oneself. He always told her: How can God forgive her if she doesn't forgive others? Keyanna recalled how she changed from those sermons Jules gave to her. She saw forgiveness on another whole level than many people would understand.

Her forgiveness was letting go of her pain and leaving it in the hands of God to judge those that caused it. By doing so, she felt free and unburdened. After the reconciliation, she and Jules got married and started their own family. Their wedding was a small private ordeal where Keyanna only had her parents, Jules's parents, and her best friend's family. She had always been a simple individual and didn't want a large crowd for her wedding. Once the ceremony was over, they headed to Paris for their honeymoon. She handpicked the district where they would stay in Paris since she was familiar with the city from the many trips her family took while she was a young girl. She could vividly recall their hotel and how nice it was decorated to their taste upon arrival. Her daughter stayed behind with Kyara while they enjoyed a week of fun activities and amazing restaurants.

The couple visited the Louvre, Versailles, and the Eiffel Tower, of course. They also visited other cities such as Lille (France) and Brussels (Belgium). She made sure she took Jules to Le Tagine, one of her favorite restaurants in Paris, as well as Val D'europe, a shopping center near Disneyland Paris.

Keyanna suddenly felt their shuttle stop. She opened her eyes and saw that they had arrived at the Couple's Nest. She couldn't believe she took all that time to reminisce about the beginning of their relationship. Jules was still sleeping like a baby on her shoulders. She gently stroked his head to wake him up. He slowly opened his eyes and sat up straight.

"We are here, my love," she whispered.

"Already?" he asked.

"Yes already. You're tired," she replied.

The driver parked at the entrance of the center and got out to get their luggage for them. Keyanna could see a concierge heading their way to greet them. She and Jules hurried to get out of the van and get their things.

"Welcome to the Couple's Nest," said the concierge. We are so delighted to have you join us for the week. Keyanna and Jules both said thank you and followed the gentleman who seemed to be in his early thirties and very fit.

He must spend a lot of his time working out when he isn't here working, Keyanna's mind wondered.

She decided to focus on the place they just entered and how cozy and nice it was decorated. She had always been a sucker for interior design and the decorating was top-notch for such a small remote place for couples. The concierge quickly checked them in and led them to their room. He, of course, gave them a little tour of the place by showing them where the amenities were and anything else they might need during their stay. The couple received their room keys and, a few minutes later, went to their suite.

"Wow!" exclaimed Jules. "This is beautiful!"

The room was decorated with beautiful wallpaper with white-on-white decor. There was some splash of bright and fun colors that broke up the white to make it welcoming and fun. Jules and Keyanna unpacked their clothes and decided to freshen up and prepare for dinner.

Before dinner, the room service came in and dropped off a plan for the next week. They looked at it quickly and saw that it would be very busy and intensive. But they decided that anything they needed to make their relationship work, they would do. An hour later, the couple headed back to the lobby where they were directed to the restaurant for dinner.

Keyanna wore a red long-sleeve sweater dress that revealed her curves and also black sandals. She wanted to accentuate her shape to make her husband's eyes focus on her. It worked. Jules's eyes had been on her ever since he came out of the bathroom and saw her already dressed. He even acknowledged it by complimenting her on how beautiful she looked. She missed that part of him who always made her feel desired and seen. Many women in a marriage feel unnoticed by their spouses and Jules had been one who made sure he saw everything (at least in the beginning). Lately, that hadn't happened much so she was loving that he was doing it again and even throwing in recognition.

The couple finally got settled at their table and decided to start the evening with a bottle of white wine. Stella Rosa Berry was ordered because Keyanna wasn't much of a drinker. Stella Rosa is one of those wines she could drink because of the low percentage of alcohol. The menu offered diverse foods that looked and sounded amazing but were also simple. Keyanna decided to order Alfredo pasta with grilled shrimp while Jules ordered the same but with steak. One could say, men never can give up on their meat.

After finishing their dinner, they took a tour by themselves of the premises to look more in-depth at the place. All Keyanna could say was that it was amazing. It was a very cozy little place filled with nice decor and, from what she could see, different areas in the activity room that couples could use during their stay. The place also had an indoor swimming pool, a massage center, and a sauna. They rounded out the tour by stopping at a small boutique close to the restaurant where Jules bought his wife a box of chocolates. Keyanna had a sweet tooth and he wanted her to have that for a little dessert since she didn't order one at the restaurant. She was thankful for the gesture. Then they retired to their room.

The couple heard a knock at their door right after they settled in to read a book. They were surprised but Jules opened the door. A different gentleman was at the door. He stated his greetings, then introduced himself as the manager of the location.

"My name is John and I will be your coach. I will be your guide during your stay," he said.

Jules shook his hands and introduced himself, while Keyanna came over and did the same.

"Nice meeting you both," said John. "While I have you both here, I wanted to inform you that we usually start the process that you have signed up for a little differently. I noticed you both have dined and retired to your room before I came to tell you about the first phase of the program. I don't know if you had a chance to look over your plan yet, but this particular requirement that I am about to explain is never put in the plan."

Jules and Keyanna answered in unison that they didn't read the plan yet and were open to the idea.

"So what is the one thing not included?" asked Keyanna.

"Ms. Keyanna, we have a separate room for one of you. For the next three days, you two will be sleeping in separate rooms. But you will be participating in all your activities and sessions together."

"What!" Jules exclaimed.

"I know you are shocked by this new development but as your coach, I promise it is one of the best steps you are taking into this healing and recovery journey," said John.

Jules nodded and decided to take the other room and leave this room for his wife, so she could be comfortable. A few minutes later, Jules found himself in a new bed and staring at the ceiling. He didn't expect this arrangement but he did want to make his marriage work. His room was next to his wife's and there was a door separating them. *If only he had a key to that door, all this feeling would go away,* he thought. He got up and decided to run a cold shower to cool himself off. You would think Keyanna was fast asleep but she just couldn't close those pretty eyes of hers. Her mind wondered also where her husband was. She wasn't allowed to know the room number. John had made sure to remind Jules not to tell her during the next three days.

Fourteen

The knock on the door startled Jules. He jumped out of bed and ran toward the door, forgetting where he was.

"Good Morning, Jules!"

"Morning Coach, long night?" Trying to rub off the sleep of his eyes, Jules yawned and responded by shaking his head.

"I am sorry about that. I am here to remind you that your day will start in an hour. Here is your schedule. See you later!"

John walked off and headed toward Keyanna's room to inform her of the same news. Fortunately, Keyanna was already up and dressed for the day. Once she heard the knock, she swiftly headed to the door and spoke with the coach. He informed her of the news and also gave her the schedule. The only difference that Keyanna didn't know was that she had been assigned to arrive a little earlier than her husband so they both wouldn't meet each other on the way out.

The couple looked forward to this day for they had no idea how things would go, but they were hopeful. John was waiting for them under the tent created for just the two of them. It was an all-white tent with two pillows that were put close to each other. John welcomed them and asked them to each sit on their pillows.

"I am very glad to have you two here and I hope that this place brings you more together and heals all those wounds that won't heal. Today, we will focus on the "Why." The "Why" focuses on the reason you both came together and have loved each other. The "Why" gives you a reason to continue trying for your union and to believe that anything great can happen in your union. The "Why" is the other word for "Forgiveness" as we say here at the center. So now it's time for the first exercise of the day called "Connect."

John went on to say, "The "Connect" process simply emphasizes your partner; you look at each other for five minutes. The rules are to not close your eyes, speak, or look away. We would like for you to connect as long as possible. I am going to set a timer and, once I nod, you can begin. Please confirm if your seats are comfortable before we begin." Jules and Keyanna confirmed with a nod and then proceeded to do the exercise.

The couple completed the exercise well and were able to continue following the instructions for four minutes before Keyanna couldn't look her husband in the eyes again. The coach took some notes and asked them how it went. The couple said that it went well and they were amazed at how great they did. The coach agreed and sent them to eat breakfast with the exception of not discussing what they saw or felt during those four minutes. They were to report back to the garden center an hour after breakfast.

Breakfast time was a bit cold between the couple. Neither of them could eat their food because they wondered what each other was feeling. They dabbled at their food and did small talk until the next meeting.

During the next session in the garden, the coach asked them to observe nature and write what they saw. This exercise was called "See." He shared the importance of "See" in one's life and others.

He explained further, "We all see things with different views. Our eyes can see the same thing but there are so many interpretations depending on the viewer. This is reflective of the saying "Beauty is in the eye of the beholder." Then an hour was allowed for the couple to journal what they saw and, afterward, they were officially free for the day. There would be a movie date that evening.

In the evening, Jules and Keyanna went to the movie and enjoyed it. Before retiring to their rooms, they ate dinner at a local eatery called "The Lost Kitchen." It is said that it hosted the likes of Martha Stewart, Oprah, and many more celebrities. Jules and Keyanna felt honored when the center told them that they had a reservation for them. They sure enjoyed their meals and loved the experience. It was definitely a place to revisit.

While retiring to their rooms, John swung back to wish the couple goodnight and made sure they followed the rules of not knowing where they both were staying. Of course, Jules knew but couldn't say a word. He wondered what that was all about. Both retired peacefully to their rooms as they shared a passionate kiss that they hadn't experienced in a while. Keyanna smiled and walked off. Somehow, she felt like a little kid inside. Butterflies were all in her belly, a feeling she at one point forgot existed.

Fifteen

The next day went by quickly. First, the couple met their coach who introduced them to Lynda. Lynda was also a coach at the Couple's Nest Center but worked with couples only when she was needed. She introduced the couples to various activities throughout the day and kept them on their toes. The first activity focused on tube riding where the couples had to trust each other to float and be each other's partners. The next activity focused on being a team player. The couple played a game with three other couples. Jules and Keyanna were put on the same team so they could depend on each other to win the game. Fortunately, their team won and they later enjoyed ice cream to cool off at the garden center while resting on the swings.

Keyanna thought the day went well because she didn't feel like any of the challenges were emotionally hard compared to their first day. She was excited and ready to see what tomorrow held. As she sat in bed, reminiscing about the day, she recalled the passionate kiss between Jules and herself. It was when the game was won. They immediately ran to each other and kissed without even realizing it until one of the couples cleared their throats. They came back to their senses and apologized for being distracted. Keyanna giggled remembering how good it felt.

In his room, Jules was wondering when he would finally spend a night with his wife. He was loving all the activities but he wanted to feel connected to his wife in a private way. He felt he was ready to be intimate again with her. He didn't know if she was ready but he was and he would work to make that happen. Due to the busy day they had, Keyanna and Jules both fell asleep quicker than they had done so in the past two days. They were looking forward to what tomorrow would bring.

The next morning, they were joined at breakfast by coach John again who wanted to spend time with them and discuss their first-day activity. The activity was called "Connect" and the parties were asked not to share what they felt during those few minutes.

"How are you all doing?" asked coach John.

"Great," they replied. "We are ready for today."

Well, I am glad to hear that," John said. "Today is an easy day. Being your third day at the center, we like to do simple tasks today. Once you both wrap up with breakfast, let's meet in my office. How about in a half-hour?"

Thirty minutes felt like a long time for the couples who didn't know what to expect next. They finished their meals quickly and were in the office before the half-hour was up. Nevertheless, coach John made sure to take his time and began at the agreed-upon time. He deliberately did that to read their body language and tell how tense they might be.

"Welcome to another session of your plan. As I shared earlier, today is a simple day. I would like to start by asking Jules to share his experience during the "Connect" session you all did. Jules, how was it and what did you learn? And is there anything else you want to share or express? Since the man remains the head of the household no matter the circumstance, I have asked that you begin, Jules."

Jules thought and then explained, "At first, I questioned how the activity would help but then, in the middle of it, I realized that it was deeper than anything I have done in a while. When the timer started, I wasn't focused at first, but then I started to focus when I kept my wife as my focal point. Looking into her eyes brought back forgotten memories and emotions that I thought were lost."

"Can you share some of those memories?" John asked.

"Yes, of course! The process took me back to the time and the circumstances we met and all the things she and I used to do as a couple. It made me remember how close we were. We shared everything and did everything together when we got together in the beginning."

John continued to ask more questions. "How did that make you feel, Jules?" asked coach John.

Jules wanted to answer quickly but he bent his head down and said sadly, "I was sad and angry at myself because I couldn't understand why the disconnect is between us now and how we ended up here."

"Don't worry too much, Jules. You being here is part of the answer to that question. What about you, Keyanna? Do you mind sharing some of your experiences with us?"

"She hesitated a little bit and then started sharing. "I was connected to him from the moment we started. The process took me back to our wedding day, the birth of our kids, and our honeymoon. Somehow, it gave me back the details that I had forgotten over the years."

John spoke, "That's great! Why do you think it took you to those exact moments? Remember there is no wrong answer here. Just be free with your response."

Keyanna added, "I'm not sure but what I can think of is that it happened because those are some of the important moments I never let go of. I am a great believer in the "Why." The why we got together, the why we married each other, and the why we needed to fight for it. Our wedding day, the birth of our children, and so forth are memories I will forever cherish. So for me, it's natural that my spirit or the exercise took me back there."

"Well, thanks for sharing. I appreciate you both being vulnerable and laying it all out there. I want to ask what each of you thought about each other's responses? The trick is that you will write those responses down and we will visit them later. A quick reminder before I let you go. You'll be meeting one of our previous participants later in the afternoon and she'll go over the "See" exercise with you. I know you wrote a lot that day and I can't wait to see how you both did and if the experience gave you something back. Now, I want to ask one more question. Jules, what do you believe that you learned from this experience?"

Jules and Keyanna both looked at each other and started to speak at the same time. Jules nodded and allowed his wife to speak.

"The experience gave me back reasons why I shouldn't leave my husband no matter what," said Keyanna.

"What about you, Jules?" John asked.

"Well, one thing I learned through that lesson is how great my wife's company used to be and how I have forgotten that. The exercise helped me to cherish and want to make more memories. So, I guess the greatest lesson learned is to work on bringing habits back into our marriage to regain our closeness."

"You both are doing great. I'm really proud of the work you have put into this for the past few days," John responded.

The couple wrapped up another session with the former participant later that afternoon. Keyanna loved Stacey. She was on point with many things they had written in their journals for "See." One thing she loved the most was her reminding them of how everyone sees things differently and that there are various interpretations. Another thing was about communication and that the key to communication isn't just talking to each other but also understanding each other and what truly the other person is saying. Keyanna loved that more than anything because she felt people tend to focus on communicating and forget the importance of understanding. Keyanna smiled and couldn't say thank you enough for this journey that they had embarked on.

Jules and Keyanna were back in their rooms but they were told that tomorrow they could return to the same room. Little did Keyanna know that the plan was to have Jules open the connecting door to her room in the evening of the next day. Jules was made aware of that tonight and he couldn't wait to hold his wife and spend time with her. He knew the wound wasn't gone but he was grateful that they were past the hurt and were now at that place where healing could occur. There was no doubt Keyanna would still have her outbursts at times for forgiveness isn't a one-day journey but Jules would be there to reassure her and use the tools they were learning now to remind her that he was here now and wouldn't make that mistake again.

Missing her children dearly, Keyanna placed a call to her parents to check on them. They were fine and happy to be staying with their grandparents. The conversation between Keyanna and her firstborn was quick because the children were playing hide-and-seek. Keyanna was just so thankful to God for her amazing children. Autistic or not, she wouldn't trade them for anything in the world. Keyanna had always felt blessed when it came to the children; they were the essence of her life and the fuel that kept her going and striving to be the best version of herself. She couldn't see her life without them. Even though the beginning of her motherhood brought nothing but pain, she was indeed grateful for the outcome. Undoubtedly, gold can never be its best unless the process of fire is used. She stayed on the phone a little longer and discussed the trip with her mother and shared how Jules and she were having fun and relaxing.

Her parents did not seem to know the details of their trip. Keyanna didn't plan to share anything on that matter with them. She saw the marital troubles as a problem between her spouse, herself, and God. Her best friend knew about it because she was always the only "sister" she had. Talking about her best friend, she recalled that she forgot to reply to her message earlier. So she called her also and they both talked late into the night.

Sixteen

The following day involved work, as usual. The couple couldn't believe it was their last day of activities with the coaches and the other participants. The remaining two days would be focused on what they chose to do and the places they could explore outside the center on their own before returning home.

They shared with their coaches and talked about their activities, the lessons learned, and how they could go back to some of these activities when difficulty arose once they got home. The coaches reminded them that healing takes time just like forgiveness takes time. They repeated some of the messages learned: You can forgive but not necessarily forget, and while you are healing, the memories of those hurt times might occur, but they should remember to take one day at a time and practice what works best for them.

The coach shared more advice with the group. "I want you all to take each day as a gift and not stress and try to create things that aren't there. Just enjoy the moment and appreciate life, your relationship, your children, and your family as a gift each day. I promise it will get better and easier when you do so. As Christians, I want you to remember also to bring Christ in the middle of it. He is the beginning and the end so He knows and sees it all. A while ago, I learned that we need Christ more for the things He doesn't need to fix for us. Let me explain that better. You see, many of us go to Christ to ask Him to fix this, do that, and be that. Yes, He willingly does it all for us, but we have to remember that most times, we just need His presence, the relationship we build with him, and the understanding that He is more than a problem solver. Rather He is who we want Him to be. "I am that I am" is said in the Bible. So hold on to that and I know you will all do just fine."

Then the coach spoke directly to the couple. "You are a great couple that still has a love for each other. I pray this experience has opened you up to see that all you need is each other and God. You have overcome so much and my prayer is happiness and more grace for you two as you continue to grow and lean on each other. Remember that you are partners before anything else. When you see your husband/wife as your partner, it's easier. When you hold each other accountable, you have each other's back and you fight for each other. Hence, balance, love, friendship, and so forth are created. On behalf of all the coaches, we want to thank everyone for trusting us."

Jules and Keyanna felt a type of rush and relief within their bodies at the same time and both ran to each other and hugged for a long time. At that moment, Keyanna knew she had let go of all that was holding her back; so did Jules. It was a new beginning, a new chance to do it right or they dared to say better than before. They were thankful. Now they had a few days for themselves and would be back together tonight. The center said that dinner would be set up for them tonight and they needed to meet with an assistant to get "beautified" before the evening.

Later on, in the evening, Jules's mouth dropped as he saw his wife walk into the restaurant. They had a reservation for two at a local and well-known restaurant in town. He was speechless for a moment and then realized he needed to run and kiss his wife. *How blessed can someone be?* he thought. I am the most fortunate man on the planet. That still voice inside him stated: *I agree!*

Keke was wearing a lovely satin gown that showed her beautiful curves. The dress hugged her a bit around her curves while leaving her attractive legs mid-bare. Brown skin was simply beautiful. She had her hair done with her natural curls hanging a few inches off her shoulders. Keyanna always had a beautiful body and hair. Tonight was no exception as if she knew her husband was going to look amazing as well. She sure set the tone. Jules was, indeed, a handsome man with his medium-dark tuxedo fitted to his body. He looked as gorgeous as ever. His masculinity was over the top and that perfume he was wearing brought out feelings that Keyanna had for him. Those were feelings she hadn't felt in a while.

Jules welcomed his wife with a lustrous kiss and pulled up the chair for her. One thing Keyanna was always thankful for was his great habit of making her feel valued and loved all the way. Jules was and remains a gentleman despite his flaws.

"*Tonight, I'm not going to focus on any of his flaws but rather, this time, I am blessed to share with him,*" thought Keyanna. They both told each other how beautiful they looked through their facial expressions. They couldn't believe that those habits came back. They had been a couple who could exchange many things just by looking at each other and apparently that bond was still there.

Their menu featured the things they loved: seafood, wine, and healthy choices. Jules had taken the liberty with the help of the center to create their menu for that night and also set up a surprise for his wife for later on that evening. Keyanna had no clue about it and he wanted to try his best to keep the secret to himself until then. The old Jules couldn't hide things from his wife even if his life depended on it and that old Jules was back and more refined, too. He smiled and Keyanna caught that.

"What is that mind of yours thinking about or plotting again?" she asked.

"Oh, nothing," replied Jules. "I just can't get over the fact of how lovely my wife looks tonight."

"Well, thank you, that means a lot to me coming from my husband," she admitted.

After two hours, the couple retired to their rooms with the intention that Jules would join Keyanna in an hour. Unknown to her, her room had been redone to fill their needs over the next two days and especially tonight. Jules had a beautiful bouquet of white lilies next to her lamp on her bed table, a plate of charcuterie, and a cheese and crackers assortment like she loved with, of course, some sweet white wine. He also had their bathroom set up with candles and in the room as well. He planned to propose all over again to his wife tonight and create a new memory for life with her. While reaching for her keys and opening the door, Keyanna turned on the light switch but held her breath when she lifted her head.

She was taken back by the sight of the room. She didn't need to ask who did all this because she realized only Jules knew she loved lilies. She even had a tattoo of them with her favorite quote from her grandmother: "Be Still and Know That I Am God." She missed this part of her husband, the thoughtful surprises, the love, care, and attention. Oh, how she was glad to have this moment back slowly. She was thankful. *Thank you, Father. I bless You for this moment*, her inner thoughts shared as a prayer to God. Keke loved making short prayers. They had become a part of her since childhood. They helped her stay calm and not lose her control in so many situations and also they reminded her that God was with her constantly. This was a habit she had also passed along to her best friend and had prayed that her girls would also inherit.

Keyanna led herself into her room and took a moment to appreciate every detail and touch her husband had added to the room. She inhaled the good from the room and exhaled the negative energy that was around these past weeks. It sure felt like a new beginning and she was taking it all in. She stepped into the bathroom and saw more surprises and just couldn't hold her excitement. She screamed out loud, an exclamation of excitement and happiness. She decided to wash up and get into a lovely nightgown for her spouse. Just as she stepped into the shower, she heard a noise. *Was her mind playing tricks on her?* She put her robe back on and headed toward the main room. To her surprise, she saw her husband standing near the other door which was wide open with nothing on but a pair of boxers and carrying some flowers in his hands. Her mind raced to how he got in, but she would figure that out later. She ran to him and gave him the longest kiss ever.

They both got entangled in each other and spent the next few hours all over themselves. Jules was blessed with another chance in this lifetime to make love to his wife as he had never done so before. He loved each part of it and could tell his wife did also. She was back to him. The way her body was responding to his touch, his aura, and body movement gave him all the reassurance in the world that this place is where he was meant to be. They spend their next hours in each other's arms, thinking of all good memories, and appreciating and truly being present in that moment. There was nothing more important than the time they were spending together now. *This is amazing and mind-blowing,* Keyanna thought. She had so much joy inside of her that she couldn't keep it in. So she showed it to her husband by holding him tight as if her life depended on it.

Surely, she fell asleep in his arms while he spent more hours watching her and just taking in all the blessings that were in front of him. *Indeed, anyone who finds a wife, finds a good thing.* He remembered that verse. *Really? Wow, God, I am not only getting my wife back but I am also coming back to you. Thank you for not letting go, thank you for always being there even when I felt lost and lonely,* he thought. He detangled himself from her arms and slowly rested her head on one of the pillows. Slowly on tiptoes with the effort not to wake her up, he took the new ring he had gotten for her. He slid it on her finger while removing the old ring. He placed a kiss on the ring and prayed that she would love it in the morning. Keyanna had always been an easy and simple person. She wasn't the type who focused on material things but rather the connection that she could build with people. So he knew that no matter what he gave her, she would be thankful. However, he wanted to go big or nothing, so he gifted her a four-carat engagement/wedding set.

Jules's intention was for them to renew their vows the next day at the center if she said yes when she woke up. He wanted to go back home to a new and redefined man and couple. He hoped Keyanna was on the same page as he was. He slid back into bed and held her till daybreak.

Seventeen

Keyanna woke up before Jules; she couldn't believe the night they had. She didn't even have the chance to freshen up or remove her makeup before falling asleep. She got up slowly and walked on tiptoes to the bathroom. She first cleaned up her makeup and took a warm long shower. She was so focused on last night in her thoughts that she didn't even realize her husband had come in and was right behind her. The only time she knew such a thing was happening was when she felt his arms around her and then she jumped out of surprise.

"Good morning, Love! Good morning, Sunshine! How are you? Hope you slept well," asked Jules.

"I had an amazing night, baby. Thank you for that," Keyanna described.

"I had the same experience and I thank you for that as well," replied Jules.

They both kissed again and helped each other shower. Keyanna still hadn't noticed anything about the ring because she was used to wearing a wedding ring. It wasn't until she started putting her facial lotion on that the mirror reminded her of the change. She screamed as she just saw a ghost and her husband came rushing.

"Jules, when did you change my ring?" she asked.

"While you were sleeping, honey. I wanted to give you a new beginning so I bought a new set. I want us to renew our vows to ourselves today before we go back home. I need you to know that you are the best thing that has happened to me and I am so happy to have you in my life," Jules told her.

Tears of joy came rushing down his wife's face and he held her so tight and kissed her. Keyanna finally finished dressing after, of course, making love to her husband that morning and deciding to share new vows between themselves in the room. Keyanna had always been extra simple and didn't care much for a crowd and "complicated things" as she would call them. She told her husband that God was with them when she saw the ring so every new vow they made today, He had it written and they also had it written in their hearts. That's why they didn't need a third party to do anything.

The first thing that attracted Jules to her, in the beginning, was her simplicity and it seemed she hadn't lost any bit of it over the years. So they exchanged new vows promising each other fidelity, love, partnership, and more with God in between. They agreed it was a brand new beginning and God with his infinite mercy and grace would guide them. They would still honor the time Jules had reserved for the ceremony by simply talking with the pastor and praying with him and, later on, eating their lunch with the other couples at the center.

They both thought that the time spent with the pastor was amazing and it was even better with the other couples who were ending their time at the Couple's Nest, too. Jules and Keyanna couldn't believe that their time was over. When they came a week ago, things were not as good as they were today. Indeed, this place was magical and felt like God's love. They sure would recommend it to anyone in need of a good place to reconnect, forgive, and more. This place was now part of their story, a story they would one day share with their children when they faced trials and tribulations of life and relationships.

"Is it funny that we as children of God go through hard times as individuals? We all have those periods where we can't handle them, but it's important to hold on to God and know that He is certainly there for us to make the problems and situations a little easier. I pray today for those who do not know the Savior yet and pray that doors open up for them to encounter Him in all his ramifications and glory. Amen," said Jules. The couple retired to their chambers and rounded up the evening talking and reflecting on what they had been through and how strong they were despite it all. God cannot forsake them, that much they knew so they would continue to trust Him and believe that He had good plans for both of them and their children as well.

Eighteen

It was the day of departure and Jules and Keyanna were en route to the airport. Their flight was in two hours. In the mindset of "better to be early than late," they wanted to be at their gate earlier. They sure made it happen. Going through security was quick because they were pre-registered through the TSA program. That program was an excellent option for it allowed those who were checking in to go through another lane which tended to be faster than the normal lane.

Once at their gate, Keyanna took out her novel *The Awakened Woman* by Dr. Tererai Trent and began reading. She had been fixated on that novel for the past few weeks. It was a good book that every woman needed to read and share with their husband.

"Are men allowed to read that book? Jules asked.

She laughed and said, "No."

He gave up but at least he tried. Jules put his own set of headphones on and started listening to some jazz. Jules was a jazzman if there was such a title for anyone. He enjoyed jazz and made it a point to not miss any hometown or sometimes out-of-state concerts. He was a big cheerleader for local talents and would often take Keyanna out to a concert so she could experience it the way he did.

Truly, his wife agreed most of the time to please him for she believed that each person in a relationship must compromise to balance the love and friendship there was between them. Some concerts Keyanna had enjoyed in the past while others weren't as much as she would expect, but having Jules beside her made the time spent worth it. Just like Keyanna, Jules tended to compromise by going on the numerous trips Keyanna loved. He wasn't a traveling person but joined her to make his wife and children happy. There was never a dull moment in the summer with his wife. She was a free spirit who would always find some type of activity for them to do. She also didn't let autism get in her way. Autism or not, her children would have fun and experience things just like any other kids. He loved her for that.

An hour later, the couple found themselves boarding their three-hour flight which was non-stop to Omaha, Nebraska. Keyanna thought that was plenty of time to listen to music and finish the last chapter of her book. Once safety procedures were explained, the plane took off. As someone who was overly cautious, Keyanna made sure of her surroundings and the exits near her and her spouse before truly settling in. For the next hour, everything seemed great and the passengers were ready to get their snacks and drinks the flight attendants had prepared for them.

Knowing there were roughly two hours left, Keyanna got up to use the restroom. Upon returning to her seat, the pilot had sent out a seat belt in place warning because of turbulence. She hurried up, got back to her seat, and buckled up. Despite that, the turbulence increased due to rough air and unexpected heavy rain. So she held onto her husband's hand. The captain notified the crew and passengers of the heavy rain that they were dealing with over the intercom. The rain wasn't predicted by the weatherman and yet it seemed to get stronger as the minutes passed by. The captain reminded everyone to stay seated and belted in.

Keyanna began praying and covering the plane with Jesus's blood as she and her husband did at the beginning when they got on the plane. She would never embark on a plane or any trip without asking for God's mighty hands to be upon it. So this time wasn't different. Prayers were made and now, at this moment and time, she began praying again with the help of her husband by her side.

The turbulence grew more intense and the plane shook because of the strong wind. Suddenly, the oxygen masks dropped. Chaos began a few minutes later. Keyanna could only hear the captain telling them to prepare for an emergency landing because the rain was getting worse and visibility was becoming an issue. The cabin was losing pressure and the pilot was losing control of the plane. She quickly put her oxygen mask on; so did Jules. Panic took over. A child was crying and so were other passengers. They, on the other hand, were holding each other without blinking an eye but speaking with their eyes while mumbling words that could only be prayers.

"I love you, Keyanna,"

"I love you, too, Jules."

"Never forget that," said Jules.

Abruptly, they noticed that the plane was going down and the next thing she recalled was a loud and unbearable noise and then all was black.

The plane had just crashed. There was total darkness everywhere. Keyanna felt her right hand was empty. Jules wasn't holding her hand anymore. She couldn't see. All she could hear were cries and they sounded distant, fainted like they were so far from her. She tried to speak but her voice wasn't loud enough.

"Jules, are you close? Jules, Jules, Jules, can you hear me, my love? Where are you? I am scared, Jules. Answer me, please. I can't see, Jules. Everywhere is dark."

She started panicking until she felt the grip of someone. "Hello, is someone there? Who just touched me?"

"Hello, yes, I'm here. My name is Nicole. I am one of the flight attendants. I can see you and can also hear you. Can you see me?" asked Nicole.

"No, I can't see anything. My eyes are open but everything is black."

"Don't worry. Don't panic, God will see us through," the attendant said in a comforting voice.

"God, oh yeah, God. Where is He right now? I would love to speak to Him and ask Him a few questions," said Keyanna. "Why would He let this happen to us? Nicole, can you help me find my husband?"

"We need to find out first where we are and then call for a rescue," said Nicole. "I don't know if there are other survivors out here but first things first. Let's get out of the plane. From what I gather, we are still in the wing of the plane, though I don't know how feasible that is. I will need you to trust me to be your guide."

"It's not like I have any choice right now; you are all I have, Nicole."

"Can you move your body?" the attendant asked.

"Yes, I think so," Keyanna answered.

"On the count of one, two, three, let's get up slowly," the attendant suggested.

Keyanna turned her body around and slowly followed the guiding steps Nicole was giving her. There was a lot of debris and very little walking space through everything. Though Nicole has been trained many times for this type of incident, this was her first time in any crash and she was very much afraid. She was holding on to God in her heart and, right now, gathering all the courage up for she had a beautiful son out there who was waiting for her to come home. She wouldn't let him lose that hope. And she was looking forward to that smile every time she got home."

So Nicole guided Keyanna through the one wing that was open to the outside. Luckily, it wasn't too difficult given Keyanna sat two rows from the wing. Nicole couldn't believe the number of people she had to push aside to have some space to walk through. She held it in but couldn't resist throwing up at some point. This was too much for her to bear. There wasn't any sign of life while she was walking. She started to scream asking if anyone could hear them. *There has to be someone other than us here,* she thought. Then she said a prayer to herself, *Lord. Please help us!*

With some difficulty, Nicole pulled Keyanna through the exit and also dragged herself out given there weren't many steps to walk. Finally, they were outside in the open.

Looking around, it seemed that they landed on an island. Nicole spotted the ocean in the distance and a thick forest surrounding them. She helped Keyanna sit down on the ground and continued checking the surroundings for a sign of life. *Where in the world were they? How much did the wind and heavy rains affect their route?* One question at a time she reminded herself.

It was survival mode time. She told Keyanna to stay put while she went around the crash site to get access to the captain's area to see if there was any hope to connect with the airline or anyone else. She checked herself first, making sure she hadn't sustained any injuries. For all she knew and wanted to believe, a rescue was on the way.

It took a while for Nicole to circle the plane while looking for any life and also to access the plane again. She finally got a better understanding of the crash and decided to climb into the cockpit to find some emergency tools. She was able to find the dispatch radio which seemed dead and not working. Then she recalled the emergency bag that was usually placed in their area. For her to access that, she needed to go back to the wing entrance they used and crawl to the back of the plane. A part of her wasn't ready for that because it meant seeing all those dead bodies again, but she ought to survive, she reminded herself. With the little courage left in her, she went back through the wing and crawled to the back. By the grace of God, she was able to gather two emergency bags and find a wool blanket and a couple of water bottles. *How is it possible that these things remained intact?* she questioned, but it wasn't the time for that.

She slowly crawled herself backward while screaming and searching for any sign of life. She threw out all that she found on the ground and returned to the plane. She wanted to crawl to the front of the plane and recheck for any sign of life again. Who knows, she may be lucky this time around. She had to crawl twice as far as she did before and, without a doubt, continue to throw up as some scenes were just too much. This was a full plane of 356 passengers. She refused to accept that only two out of those people were alive. There had to be someone in here. With one of the flashlights she found, she began her way up only to be stunned by a small, fainted cry. She thought she was hallucinating but she continued and crawled toward the cry. The more she headed that way, the cry was more vivid. She stopped to move bodies to the left and right just to see where that particular noise was coming from. To her surprise, she came across a baby.

"Oh, Jesus," she said. She rushed to bring the baby out of the pile of dead bodies that surrounded her. It was a precious beautiful baby. She couldn't recall having any mother on board that had a baby but right now; that was the least of her problems. She was just thankful that she took the time to recheck the plane for any survivors. If not, this precious soul would have been lost. She carried the baby in her arms and crawled backward her way out this time. With truly no strength remaining, she fell on the ground but held on to the baby with all the strength she had. She yelled out Keyanna's name.

Keyanna responded with a fearful tone of voice and began moving her hands in different directions to try to touch her or hold her.

"Keyanna, I am not close to you so you can't touch me. I found a baby while going through the plane for emergency kits and other supplies. I think she, you, and I are the only survivors on this island. I was able to gather some emergency kits and a wool blanket, but the communication tools are dead so I can't reach anyone. Please try and walk straight to me. I am facing you but don't have any strength to come to you yet," Nicole spoke directly.

Listening to Nicole's voice, Keyanna slowly walked toward it and was able to touch her hands. She sat down next to Nicole who handed the child to her. With all the remaining strength in her, Nicole opened up the bags and found useful things that could help them in the next day or two.

The bag contained a flashlight, crackers, canned food, Band-Aids, and bottles of water, too. Nicole drank some water and gave some to Keyanna and the baby. She told Keyanna that they seemed to have water around them and a thick forest behind them. She also found a firecracker that might help the rescuers locate them and one emergency light that she could create a triangle with as a sign of despair. Nicole then slowly walked to the shore and washed her face and hair with the water. She knelt down for a while on the ground while connecting to Mother Earth. She needed to come back to herself because what she saw in the plane gave her so much fear.

Though she was a Christian, Nicole still connected to her roots, traditions for she believed without them, one was lost. She knew the power of the soil, so she touched it as a way to reconnect to nature and all the forces of it, asking for strength and help for this new challenge of her journey that she had just begun. After a while, Nicole reconnected to herself and walked back to Keyanna to help her by guiding her to the water, washing her face, and giving her time to feel better. Keyanna sat there lost as she washed her face and didn't even know what to think at the time. The loud cry of the baby brought her back to reality. She then sought the help of Nicole and was brought back ashore.

There Nicole set up a small space with a blanket, food, and the water they had gathered. She also tried to clean up some scratches she had on herself and also Keyanna and the baby. Looking around and seeing that darkness was lurking, she decided to go find some wood and stones to start a small fire to keep any animals away and also to cook the canned foods. She left the baby in Keyanna's care. Somehow, Keyanna noticed that the saltwater helped her vision a bit. She could see faintly but wasn't sure why and how she suddenly lost her sight. *Is this what life has in store for me? Blind and a widow? How is it that life can change in a split second?* She refused to believe in these changes that were happening too fast in her life. *Jules, where are you? If you can feel me or hear me, please come to me. Please answer me. I can't do this without you. You are my everything and more.* Small teardrops ran down her cheeks and fell on the innocent baby. She just wanted to feel, hear, or see her husband, her kids, and her parents.

How are they feeling right now? she thought. *I am sure they heard of the crash;, they will be panicking and anxious at this moment and time.*

How will I tell the kids about Jules? No, Jules isn't dead. He is alive, just probably passed out under another passenger. Jules will come back to me; I truly believe that.

In a short time, Nicole returned with some wood and stones. She quickly set up a fire and cooked the beans and vegetables found in the emergency kit. Nicole was very thankful to her dad who taught her Surviving 101 in the forest. Not knowing that, she wouldn't have made it so far today. She admitted that she was scared on the inside but she had always been a person who hid her emotions pretty well. Not only that, but also it was a good thing, especially in this situation where stress was running high. This side of her was helping to keep the outward overt reactions away.

A few moments later, Nicole and Keyanna were able to eat and also drink some water. They were still hopeful that they would be found soon. They were more worried about the baby. Nicole had to do another round in the plane to look for formula or anything they could feed the baby with but there was no hope. So she prayed over the water and gave it to her hand-to-mouth. This was a technique that she recalled her great-grandmother doing to her cousins when they were babies and wouldn't feed on the bottle. Thankfully, the baby drank the water and, somehow, was back to her playful self.

Dark was setting in and the temperature got colder. Keyanna and Nicole didn't have much to say; you could tell their minds, hearts, and souls were heavy. The emotions they were feeling were so much, a person could sense this miles away. They managed to wrap the baby well and lay it down on the blankets they had found. Nicole shared a prayer and reminded both of them that God was in control. She truly believed that they would be found.

Nineteen

The sound of the waves mixed with the baby cries jolted them from their sleep. Keyanna couldn't believe she had finally fallen asleep. Throughout the entire night, her mind was just pacing left to right wondering about her family, husband, and so much more. Nicole seemed to have slept like a baby.

"Good Morning!" Nicole said.

"Morning, Nicole," greeted Keyanna. "How are you able to sleep so sound given our situation?"

"I am worried as much as you are but I have learned to worry less and pray more in all situations I have found myself in. Yes, the situation we are in isn't ideal. There are so many dead people right across from us and we have a baby here who hasn't eaten all day yesterday and who is probably going to become an orphan. You have become a widow overnight and I can't wait to see my son who is with my elderly mother. Trust me, I am anxious but I try to keep calm because it will do me no good otherwise," Nicole answered.

"So you have a son?" Keyanna asked.

"Yes, I do. He is five years old and autistic with a speech delay. So I have a lot on my plate. Nevertheless, I see him as a blessing. He has taught me so much; he the most gifted and pure human being.

Do you have kids," asked Nicole?

"I do," replied Keyanna, trying to hold back the tears. "I have two beautiful girls and a son. Surprisingly, my first two were both on the spectrum as well. Isn't it coincidental that the two of us who are survivors of a plane crash have children that are on the spectrum? God, I am telling you, knows best, and his ways at times aren't always how or what we think or see. I believed in all that but right now, my heart can't accept that."

"You are in shock and your body, mind, and soul are processing a lot right now. Give yourself grace, Keyanna," Nicole said in a comforting voice.

Nicole got up and went to give the longest hug to Keyanna who was crying so hard at this point.

"I am here with you and I know we will be found. The baby is still asleep, so I want to use this time and see if I can find any other food here or any sign of life. Do you need anything before I go?" Nicole asked.

"No, I'll be fine."

"Okay, here is the baby. I'd rather you hold her in your arms because you still have trouble seeing. This way, we are just being cautious."

At the Omaha airport, Keyanna and Jules's family were waiting to speak to anyone who could provide any news about the flight that had recently crashed. They got tired of calling and being passed down from one person after the other over the phone. So they went to the airport demanding answers. Upon arriving at the airport, it seemed like they weren't the only ones. The airport lobby was filled with people asking questions about the Pacific Airlines Flight 1458. Pacific Airlines is a very reputable airline and many people trusted them; with this crash, they might lose a lot of customers if things weren't handled properly. The airline crash had been on every local and national channel you turned on these past few days. For Keyanna's grandparents, keeping the grandkids from the news was already a hard chore. And thinking something terrible happened to their own children (Keyanna and Jules) was another hard chore for both sets of parents.

For the next few hours, Keyanna's parents and Jules's father sat at the airport. Finally, they were approached by the general manager on duty who shared with them that they were doing everything possible to locate the crash. He further stated that the crash location was identified via satellite and they were gathering a team to head out there.

The manager explained, "Given what we saw, the unexpected heavy rains and wind rerouted the plane which changed its course, hence causing the crash and making the pilot land on an island. The island that we believe the plane happened to crash on is Peddocks Island which is one of the Boston Harbor Islands. More updates will be shared as our team gets on the ground. I am truly sorry about all of this but trust that we are working day and night to bring all our passengers back home."

"Have you been able to reach anyone on the crew?" asked Keyanna's father.

"No, we haven't. That's one reason we are rushing to get there as soon as possible."

He explained more information to those gathered in the airport. "Our team is getting ready as we speak. I would please ask that you all go home and wait for more news. We will be reaching out to you individually once on the ground. Thank you so much and, once again, we apologize for everything."

Keyanna's parents and Jules's father didn't know what to say or how to feel. They headed back home and hoped and prayed that their children would be found soon. The only thing they knew how to do was pray and they continued to do so for their kids and those on board as well.

Nicole was able to find some fruit and coconuts to her surprise. She was very thankful for this. However, there was no sign of life to her knowledge. She wanted to keep her hopes up high and believed that there would be a light at the end of the tunnel. She missed her son so much and her mother would be so worried. She tried not to overthink and headed toward Keyanna and the baby.

"So I have decided to name the baby. We can't keep calling her "baby." For now, let's call her Grace if that's okay with you," Nicole said.

"Sure!" Keyanna smiled.

"How is she holding up?" Nicole wondered.

"Well, given she hasn't had real food till now, I would say great. I am just worried that she won't be able to hold up longer," Keyanna said.

"Looking at Grace, I think she is definitely over nine months or so, maybe older. We can try and give her this almost-ripe banana that I found in my search through the forest."

"How come you are so brave, Nicole?"

"I wouldn't say brave but trained. I grew up watching my dad master the art of nature at every camping trip we went on. Given I was his only child, he passed on those skills to me, so I could say I am at peace when surrounded by pure nature. It doesn't worry or stress me out. This doesn't mean I'm not scared, but I have learned to adapt to it over the years. I now enjoy doing the same trips with my son," Nicole paused.

Her thoughts took her back to her son and how he must be feeling right now. She trusted her mother was doing a great job keeping him at peace and not worrying, but her mother might be devastated and wouldn't know how not to show it. Ever since her father died, Nicole's mother had never been the same. She learned how to accept the loss over the years but the light that Nicole saw during her youth in her mother's eyes wasn't there anymore. She often found her mother just dazing into space and her mind wandering from time to time when she visited for the weekends. She had suggested for her mom to move in with her, but she insisted on staying in the home she and her husband had lived in.

"Keyanna, I'm sorry, my mind wanders a bit. I was thinking of my son and my mother."

"No worries, Nicole, I am constantly thinking about my children, my parents, and my husband who I refuse to believe is dead. I just feel useless because I can't see and go look for him myself."

"Don't worry," reassured Nicole. "We will find him once help gets here. For now, let me help you wash your face to freshen up, and let's feed Grace a little bit of banana and water again."

Keyanna freshened up and just like the day before, she noticed that she could see a little bit more of her surroundings and nothing seemed as dark. She thought the stress was taking a toll on her so she just tried to ignore it. She refused to believe she was blind though, just like she refused to accept her husband's death and disappearance.

While rocking Grace after her feeding, Keyanna discovered that she could see baby Grace. Her beautiful face was smiling at her and cooing. Truly her stress had dealt with her, or maybe it was the shock from the crash. She couldn't explain anything right but was thankful for her sight coming back to her. She turned around and could see Nicole for the first time as well. She was a beautiful woman who had a caramel skin tone. Nicole was busy eating fruit.

"Nicole, I can see you!" Keyanna shouted.

"What? For real? Do you mean it?" Nicole shouted back.

Nicole ran to Keyanna, touching her face and you could see her excitement as if she had just won the lottery.

"What's my hair color, Keyanna?"

"It's blonde."

"Thank you, Lord, for this miracle. We are waiting on more from Your Father. Help us get out of here," whispered Nicole.

She was known for whispering throughout the day as she loved saying short prayers. The power of one-word or sentence prayers was just as powerful as a longer prayer she believed. She had seen the manifestation of God in her life through those prayers so she would never give up on them.

They hugged for so long. They found themselves singing to a song that Nicole hummed out of her happiness when Keyanna was able to see. It was a song titled "Jireh" by Elevation Worship. Nicole had fallen in love with the song a couple of months back when she heard it and just couldn't get over it.

Keyanna didn't hum to the tune of it. Although today felt a little bit better than yesterday, deep inside she was a wreck. Her hubby, children, family, all of that not within her reach. She would have never thought a day in her life would come to this. It's true when they say: "A moment can change a million after." What she would give to be with everyone that she loved right now.

Twenty

Nicole's mom had decided to reach out to some of her daughter's friends to see if they could get a better answer from the airline on the whereabouts of her child. She was frustrated with how long it was taking to get through to the airline. She dialed Stephanie, the one and only friend her daughter had kept through the years. Upon the first ring, Stephanie picked up and exchanged greetings with her. Stephanie shared how she called the airline herself and even told Nicole's mom that she tried to reach her, too. She replied by saying that she was on the phone for a long time and that might be why she didn't get through.

Nicole's mother Elena was one of those moms who still used their house phone for everything. She had refused the technology in her home and wanted to be tech-free. So, obviously, her landline phone couldn't have noticed Stephanie's missed calls. Either way, she was thankful Stephanie was on the line now. She shared with Elena how she has been informed that a rescue team was on its way and more news would be provided soon. Relief came through Elena. She believed with everything in her that Nicole was alive and that the precious blood of Jesus would cover her. She just knew it; call it a mother's intuition or whatever it may be. Her faith wouldn't be shaken for she served a living God and He would protect her child for her own sake and for Brice's sake. God had to do that miracle for them.

"I am thankful for your call, Stephanie," Elena said. "I have turned off the television because I don't want to scare Brice, though he probably doesn't understand all of it. I still want to protect him from any trauma. I'm convinced Nicole will return soon to him, safe and sound."

"Alright, Ms. Elena. I will call later to check on you both. Let me know if you need anything and I will come right away."

"Thank you, dear. We appreciate you, Stephanie."

"Anytime," Stephanie reassured her.

The second day seemed to have gone too fast. Nicole, Keyanna, and Grace were laying down on the sand when a loud noise jolted them from their catnap. Keyanna jumped and wondered what it was. Nicole followed her and looked up to see a plane and some helicopters. She shouted so loudly. "Yes, yes, and yes! I knew they hadn't forgotten about us. It was just a matter of time," Nicole shouted.

Keyanna felt a rush of relief. She wanted to go to the plane crash site and search the plane for her husband all day long but Nicole had prevented her from going. Nicole did all that she could because she didn't want Keyanna to see the number of bodies lying around and the decapitation of some of them. That's a trauma she'd rather keep to herself and not have another person experience it.

A moment later, a helicopter circled overhead and noticed the sign Nicole had made on their arrival to the island. Today, that particular sign helped the helicopters land. There were four helicopters and one airplane that made their landing on the water near the shore. The pilots landed with such perfection that Keyanna was impressed. Given the island was small and the crash was still on the ground, the crew had to know how to work their way around it so they would have space to do the work they came for.

As soon as they hit the ground, the crew members were coming out of the aircraft as quickly as they could. One of them introduced himself to Nicole after walking over to her. Nicole took the liberty to explain what happened and how they had been managing the past two days. She shared her thoughts of the plane and assessment and believed that there probably weren't any more survivors. Caleb, the chief in charge, nodded. He then rallied his team and gave the instructions needed to start the search. Prior to that, some water and baby formula were mixed for Grace who gulped it down in a few moments. Despite being relieved, Keyanna kept wondering when they would bring her husband out of the plane.

It could take days for this nightmare to be over. On a positive note, there was a plane ready to take them to the Boston Airport, and then they would be looked after before arrangements were made for them to return to their homes. All of that news sounded great to Keyanna and Nicole. However, Keyanna bluntly cut off Caleb before he could share all of the news.

"I'm not leaving without my husband. I will stay here with you all until my husband is found. There is no way in hell that I'm going to leave him behind. I know he's alive and in there; I refuse to believe he is dead. He may be injured but not dead."

Nicole came closer to Keyanna and rubbed her shoulder to give her some relief: A message that we are all here with you and for you.

The crew members had nurses and a doctor with them, so they camped out and looked after Nicole, Keyanna, and Grace. Keyanna showed no signs of injury and Nicole only had some scrapes on her forehead. The doctor thought it was a miracle with the type of crash that happened. Anyone could see the damage to the plane. Somehow, the crash split the plane into three and one wing was still missing from what they had uncovered so far. Maybe the wind had carried it away from them or maybe it was in the ocean. Either way, it would be found. Grace showed no sign of starvation or sickness or injury. Instead, she seemed to be very happy and at ease with both ladies. After being checked by the doctor, they were given new clothing, shoes, and other things they needed.

The sun was going down and the search wasn't nearly halfway finished. Keyanna and Nicole had a chance to make a call to their relatives and, of course, the news station hadn't shared anything yet with the public although they came an hour ago to the island to confirm that the search was being conducted. A great relief came to Nicole's mother and Keyanna's parents. But Jules's father was still uneasy because his son hadn't been found yet. Keyanna reassured him that she wasn't leaving without her partner. She would join the search if they allowed her to do so and help find her husband. Nicole had decided to leave with the first passengers that the crew had taken out of the plane. There was a count of 100 passengers so far and all of them are dead. It seemed like the numbers were far from being over. The search started six hours ago and Caleb had no idea yet about how many bodies they may have found in the forest.

Keyanna was impressed. The crew knew their jobs and were very coordinated. They set up ways that made identifying and wrapping the bodies to be quick and effective. She had to stand by the workstation to make sure the people weren't her husband. So far, the crew had only gone through the front part of the plane, so she refused to let her hope and faith die now.

"*Oh, wow!*" the voice said. "*You still believe, Keke.*"

"Yes, I do. I am just all over the place with my faith and belief right now. A part of me is questioning God while the other is asking Him for a miracle."

Oh, please keep my husband alive for me. That still voice was one thing that kept her going amidst the hard times and she believed that each and every person had it. Keyanna thought that if you could trust that voice, work on it, and have the spirit of discernment with it, you could always overcome anything. To Keyanna, that voice was God speaking. It was our conscience talking to us and it was also our intuition.

One crew gathered the passengers on board, helped Nicole and Grace board, and prepared for departure. The other crew who had set up the tents when they first came took their break for the day. They retired to their tents after a nice warm meal made with ingredients they had brought and cooked over firewood. Keyanna found herself saying goodbye to Nicole and thanking her for everything.

They had shared contacts and promised to check on each other from time to time. That moment of goodbyes brought a lot of tears. It seems as if they had known each other all their lives. These past days taught them several things for sure: The will of God is surely not their will and God is faithful in all of His ways even if those ways may not always be what we want.

Twenty One

The plane arrived at Boston Airport with the media and family waiting patiently for answers. It had been an exhausting day but Nicole was grateful they made it. She was escorted through another gate with Grace while the media questioned more members of the airline. She knew that the families would be asked to come and identify their relatives and work on the process of releasing their bodies to them. That procedure was a very complicated and long one and she truly felt for all those passengers and their families. She still couldn't believe God had kept her safe through this crash. Caleb had asked her to keep Grace for now until the investigation and search were finished. She willingly agreed to it. She loved children and was sad when she learned Brice was the only one she could have.

Once checked into her hotel room, Nicole bathed Grace, fed her, and put her to bed. She then did the same for herself and took the time to call her mother and son. She was overjoyed to hear her little one's voice and felt blessed and grateful for this new change. She was given another chance, a chance she wouldn't take for granted. She would use it to serve and be there for others. She felt this change was some sort of wake-up call. She couldn't explain everything yet but that deep still voice was telling her better and amazing things were on the horizon coming her way. Her grandmother used to tell her that in every bad situation, blessings and good things come out of it. Nicole believed in that. This crash had taken a lot of lives but it could also be a bigger blessing or miracle for something new.

Back at the crash site, things were quiet. Everyone had fallen asleep. Tonight, Keyanna was determined. She had a plan, a plan no one knew about and she didn't want them to know either. It was her plan and she would execute it for her own satisfaction. She had to find her husband; she couldn't wait any longer. Nicole wasn't here keeping watch on her anymore and, with the crew dead asleep, she finally had a perfect time. She wanted to take time and go through the plane herself. She had been determined for a lot of situations in her life but this particular one was more than her life. It was her mission. Nothing was going to stop her.

Keyanna carefully exited her tent and headed toward the plane. She slowly climbed the wooden steps the crew had created to access the wing side where she and her spouse had sat nearby. She turned on her flashlight and slowly started to walk through the thin alley that was created earlier today by the crew once they were able to remove some bodies. She surely was thankful for that alley; given Nicole had shared before how she had to crawl to access the safety bags. Keyanna managed her way toward the place where she and Jules had sat. She couldn't believe the number of bodies that were laying around. At some point, she threw up from the nauseating smell. *How can this happen to all these people?* She was hurting so badly for her husband but also for all those who lost their lives in this crash. She sat there looking around her and all she could see was death. She found herself vomiting more and wishing for a miracle.

If only God could bring back everyone to life, and just not let the plane crash, they all would have been home right now, doing their daily routines and activities. How she missed her girls. She would give up anything just to spend time with them and Jules right now. She continued looking around the plane again in the hopes to find her husband. She was calling out his name and scavenging through the bodies and moving them around with the faith and hope that he was somewhere stuck under another body or two. Keyanna didn't realize that while searching for her spouse's body, she was also sobbing softly under her breath. The scenery was definitely not the greatest, and just the thought that she was doing this made her sick to her stomach.

A bathroom break woke Caleb up and, after using the restroom, he noticed a faint, distant light near the plane. He thought that was bizarre but still decided to follow it out of curiosity. Upon reaching the plane, he saw someone way out the back crying with a flashlight in their hands and their head between their legs. The person wasn't standing or sitting, but rather the person was in a bent position and crying very loudly.

Caleb summoned the courage and asked, "Who are you? What are you doing here?"

For all he knew, this may be a ghost or a survivor. Though he wouldn't admit it at that moment, Caleb was frightened but kept his cool. No one responded, so he started walking slowly toward the person. Keyanna finally felt the presence of someone and jolted.

"Caleb?"

"Keyanna? What on earth's name are you doing here? You were supposed to be resting in your tent."

"Well, I couldn't sleep. Actually, I haven't slept for days now. Knowing my husband hasn't been found yet made me lose sleep. I felt like a part of me has been gutted out and the worst fear was that this happened while I was awake all along. I couldn't help but to come and search for my husband alone. I know he isn't dead and is surely in here with injuries."

"I empathize with you, Keyanna. We will continue the removal of bodies and also the search tomorrow and I promise we will find him whether here or on the coast. We aren't giving up on him nor are we on the others. Now, please let's get you back to your tent."

Twenty Two

Keyanna and Caleb walked back to their individual tents and somehow sleep slowly crept in on her and she finally fell asleep. It was almost mid-day when Keyanna woke up. She utilized the common phone available to talk with her parents and the girls. She missed the girls so much but was thankful that she got to finally speak with them after so many days. She was thankful that her parents had been caring for them for this long. Keyanna could vividly recall her pregnancy days with her firstborn. When she shared the news of her pregnancy with them, they felt betrayed and saw her as a mistake, a shame, or even a failure. She came home for spring break that week and thought it was best to tell them the news. At that time, she didn't even know anything about having a child. She just knew that the same day she had lost her virginity, along came pregnancy.

Being a child who was always honest, she didn't think lying to her parents about such things was right. Little did she know that she was going to get the cold treatment and even worse. Her news came to them on a faithful Tuesday morning after breakfast. Keyanna would never forget their faces that day. Yet she held onto courage and told them the truth anyway. Her parents only had two questions for her that day: Who was the father? and Is she going to keep the pregnancy? She thought at that moment that the questions were ludicrous but she answered them anyway. Then the room became very quiet, so quiet for hours that she had to leave and visit Kyara, her best friend who was in town visiting her family as well.

The next day, Keyanna was summoned by her parents who gave her the ultimatum to abort the child or face the pregnancy on her own. Her mother told her that the child was a shame for it was conceived out of wedlock. Given their status in the church and her father's tradition, they couldn't entangle themselves in such a shame. She advised her to abort the child and face her studies. Once done with her degree, she could then marry and build her family. Tears and tears were the only things that were coming from Keyanna that day. She had lost the ability to speak or say anything. Her life and destiny had changed that day or it began that particular day. What dumbfounded her the most was her father's attitude toward the whole thing. He let her mother make decisions as usual as if he wasn't the man of the house. Keyanna had always thought her mother was a dictator when it came to certain family decisions and the way she took care of the family. As a young girl, she had always promised herself to do better by her husband rather than what her mom did by her husband.

For Keyanna, she thought families should make decisions together and when parents were challenged with their children's problems, they ought to make decisions together. One parent shouldn't have all the say. Deep within her, she knew her dad would have wanted her to keep the child. She just didn't understand why he had become a very quiet man over the years. When she was a child, he wasn't like that. He had authority and respect as a man of the house but all that changed after her tenth birthday. It was as if the world had closed in on him. He became a man who was guided and led by a woman, a woman who was so mean if truly described. To be honest, Keyanna now realized that same year her mother had changed, too. She used to be this wonderful happy being. But after that year, she slowly became so venomous of some sort and was only focused on keeping a certain image that swallowed Keyanna's relationship with her.

Thinking of it now, Keyanna wondered what could have happened. Maybe something did but she was too young to comprehend. She now wondered if she could change so much, too. A shout at the door brought her back to reality. It was Caleb.

"Come on in," Keyanna said.

Caleb let himself in and greeted Keyanna. After exchanging their greetings, Caleb proceeded to tell Keyanna how they had removed all the passengers from the plane. They had a count of two hundred this time around, making it three hundred and three including her, Nicole, and Grace.

"Are you able to come and identify your husband?" he asked.

"What about the other passengers?" she asked. "You shared before that the flight has three hundred and fifty-six passengers. So that's fifty-three who remain unfound."

"Yes, Keyanna. Though the search in the plane has been conducted, we still have to search the entire island for the remaining passengers. We're also thinking of the ocean but, as you know, the ocean will always eventually bring forth a body."

She took a deep breath, stood up, and walked out toward the tent created for the dead passengers. She had asked to put a mask and gloves on before entering the tent. She began assessing one body after another. This whole process would take longer because they had two hundred passengers all wrapped up. Never in her life did she think such a thing would occur but here she was, ready to identify Jules's body.

Jules can't be dead. He will come back to me. I know he isn't among these people. I can feel it in me. My husband is alive.

She continued scanning the many faces on the tables. One by one, she went through them and didn't find her husband. This whole thing was one of the most difficult things she ever had to do but she was thankful the Holy Spirit aided her. Though she was convinced her husband was alive, the flesh was still flesh. She was still scared so, for the first time after this tragedy, she prayed before entering the room. Her prayer was simple: "Holy Spirit, please help me."

"As I told you, Caleb, and will continue to tell you, my husband isn't dead. He might be nowhere to be found right now, but I know he isn't dead and we will find him."

Caleb stared at her and wondered about her conviction. He had never seen anyone who maintained a conviction in similar circumstances like Keyanna did. He actually had become fond of her through the many little chats they had shared over these past two days. He yearned to know more about her and just wished he could talk to her. She seemed like a woman who had her share of difficulties but overcame them and now feared nothing. If only as a man he could have such courage and faith, his life would be so much better. Keyanna walked out of the tent and breathed in the fresh air after removing her mask. It was much needed. She also grabbed some water and decided to walk a bit around the island. Ever since she regained her sight back, she hadn't gone to many other places on the island beyond the plane site.

Keyanna notified a search member and started her stroll along the shore. She found herself drawn to the many trees that surrounded the island and the beauty of the ocean afar. The waves repeatedly rolled back and forth and crashed. Each wave had a different stroke, showing you the beauty of God's handiwork. She was a walker because it connected her to the universe and God. Throughout the walk, she acknowledged God more and saw his majesty and mightiness in everything. While daydreaming, Keyanna didn't realize how far she had gotten. A soft moan brought her attention back to reality.

What's that sound?

She slowly followed the sound and screamed out loud, "Is someone there? Can you hear me?"

The moan became louder. A few steps away, when she finally lifted her head up, she saw the missing wing of the plane.

She rushed toward it, then paused to think first. This could be dangerous. Let me go back and alert the team.

"Oh, I have a walkie," she said. It was something the rescue squad gave her before she left for the stroll. She managed to use it and was able to reach them. They shared the information back and forth and then she walked back to the group in hopes to meet them halfway. A few minutes later, the crew followed Keyanna to the scene. They rushed quickly and carefully began searching the site for passengers. This part of the plane had really been broken into pieces. Trees went through the plane and some were toppled on it. It took nearly an hour for the team to remove or cut parts of them so they could have access to the wing.

Keyanna felt like a small child who was expecting a beautiful gift on her birthday. A string of hope sprung through her because she believed her husband would be found here. They wouldn't give her access to the scene that they created around the wing, so she patiently waited. An hour later, Caleb asked Keyanna to retire to her tent for a warm meal and rest but she wouldn't budge and go for that idea. She chose to remain firm there until everything was finished. She had found a sitting area where she also had the chance to admire nature in all its beauty.

The island was beautiful and had a lot to offer. The only thing was that no one lived on it. They hadn't seen any signs of life till now and she didn't think they would before they departed the island. More hours went by before the search crew started bringing out the passengers. They were able to find thirty more passengers who had lost their lives. The crew took care of them as they had done for the others and Keyanna took her time to inspect them to see if her husband was one of them. This process was draining the life out of her more and more, but she would do anything for Jules. She just wondered if her husband would ever be found.

Twenty Three

Today, Nicole finally got the chance to return to her family and she was so excited about it. Though she was a great believer of "the same car that hit you, is the one that will escort you to the hospital." This was a parable her grandmother used to say in many situations. Nicole refused to adhere to that this time around and took the train route. She still had Grace in her care until the search was completely finished. The airline didn't want to give Grace to any social services agency until all was clear. Nicole must admit, she had fallen in love with Grace. She was just an easy baby and everyone who came to know her would love her. She and Grace boarded the train heading to Atlanta. There would be some stops along the way but she was alright with that plan. After all, she could enjoy the great scenery and see the beauty of God's handiwork along the route.

Sophie ran into the living room demanding the whereabouts of her parents. It's as if she knew something was wrong. Though her speech had gotten better, she still struggled sometimes with it and she needed redirection with words at times.

"I want Mommy and Daddy," she said to her grandmother.

"Sweetheart, I know you miss your parents. I do, too. Don't you worry, they will be back soon. Let me try and connect you with your mom so she can talk to you. Brigitte had access to a line where Keyanna could be reached so she tried that line and, luckily, she was connected to Keyanna.

Keyanna spent almost an hour talking with not only Sophie but her other children. They gave her great joy and, though she knew Sophie could sense something, she tried so hard to hide it from her. She shared with them that their dad had stepped out to the store. Sophie was autistic but one of her greatest strengths had always been emotions. She could sense things from far away. She had the ability to feel everyone's emotions who were around her and bring them her own comfort. She told her mom that she loved her so many times. Keyanna had to end the call so she wouldn't cry. Keyanna was thankful that in the midst of chaos, there were three great human beings who could still put a smile on her face. How blessed could she be?

Back at Jules's father's house, the news was on 24/7 because Beau didn't want to miss a thing. He knew from his last talk with Keyanna that the search was still on, so there was hope. Jules's father was an elder who continuously shared with whoever wanted to know that his time to go to his eternal home was near. Ever since the loss of his wife, Jules could barely get his father out to do anything. He didn't seem to have an interest in anything.

All he cared for was his daily words and relationship with God. He was a devoted Christian and did everything for his son not to be astray. Jules grew up in a household of Assembly of God and had parents who loved each other dearly. He had a great example growing up and looked up to his father for everything. Though something changed in him when he lost his mother to breast cancer, Jules was a wonderful man. His father's pride was that he was the only surviving son.

Beau and his wife Brenda had two sons throughout their forty years of marriage but sickness took Jules's elder brother Caleel at the early age of two. He suffered at that time of fever that later was known as yellow fever; he didn't make it after a three-day period. They were in Congo, Kinshasa doing ministry work for the kingdom. Caleel was born in Congo and delivered by some devoted local nurses. Given that Brenda was originally born in Congo, she felt at ease with her own. She spoke French and Lingala. Her parents made sure of that despite the fact that she grew up in the United States. Beau was always fond of his wife and her ability to connect with others easily. She was a natural and she helped him become more social than he was in his younger age. He would pay anything to the world just to see her one more time. Her last days weren't the best. That beast of disease took all the strength Brenda had in her. It left her so fragile. It was so hard for him to see his wife suffer and there was nothing more he could have done about it.

Brenda was diagnosed with ovarian cancer when it was small according to the doctor. They even got a second opinion before they proceeded to have the surgery. They prayed and fasted about it and believed God was with them. So when the surgery was a success, they were happy. Brenda came home and was scheduled for a small round of chemotherapy after a month of recovery. That one month of recovery went quickly and she was back as if nothing ever happened to her. Beau was so happy. Then that fateful night before the therapy began, she had gone to take a nap and never woke up again. He recalled vividly going to wake her up for supper and her body was so cold. He then knew she had passed. The next hours felt like a tsunami had hit him. He slept by her for the entire night before Jules arrived the next day.

It was Jules who called 911 that day and helped Beau take the body to the morgue. It was also Jules who helped his father clean up and he also did the cooking for him the next day and the following days. It took everything out of Beau to find strength and arrange his wife's funeral. They had ordered an autopsy for it was strange for her to pass that way. The report came back normal. Brenda didn't suffer from anything. It was a natural death. Beau wanted to blame something or someone, but the results didn't give him that chance. For a long time, he blamed God. It was God's fault. How could He let his wife leave that way? They still had so much to do and life was unbearable without her. He couldn't manage anything without her. Brenda was his life. She understood him more than anyone; she was his confidant and his backbone. Still, until today, Beau has felt as if a part of him had been ripped off.

The loud home phone ring jerked him back to reality.

"Hello!"

"Hi Beau, it's me Keyanna."

"How are you, honey?"

"I am hanging in there and hope you are, too."

"Yes, I am," replied Beau. "Any news?"

"Well, the search team has found a lot of bodies but they aren't done yet. I am still hoping we will find Jules soon. I know my husband isn't dead. He is somewhere unconscious but alive."

Beau quieted down for a while before rejoining the conversation.

"I am hopeful, too, Keyanna. God will see us through. I want to believe He will bring back Jules, but my heart aches so much that I can't see it happening. You know, Keyanna, after the death of Brenda, I felt I was better off dead than alive. I didn't want to do anything and a part of me fell into depression."

Beau continued talking. "It was Jules and my grandchildren that brought life back to me. You had no idea at that time but the kids' visits helped me stay connected to myself, God, and life without even trying. I know we are currently going through hard times but I also know God is faithful and He will not let harm come our way. We are promised eternal and good life, but we aren't promised a trouble-free life. As children of God, the devil will always bring trouble, trials, and tribulations our way, but the grace of God will always prevail. It did for me then; I am sure it will for us again this time around."

Keyanna thanked Beau for his comforting words and promised to keep him updated.

Twenty Four

Nicole's train was closer to home than before. They had been riding for hours now and she couldn't wait any longer to reach her destination. She wanted to embrace Brice and love him. She couldn't wait to show him Grace, as well. He would be so thrilled to have a baby in the home. Brice had always asked for another sibling but Nicole had explained to him the best way she could that Mommy couldn't have any more babies. He somewhat understood in his little mind but still asked from time to time. She was blessed to have Brice. She could recall the day she found out she was carrying him. Nicole was told at her younger age when she developed PCOS (Polycystic Ovary Syndrome) that she would not be able to have children so Brice was her little miracle.

She went to the hospital that day for a checkup which turned out to be good news. Of course, at the time she wasn't married but was happy to be able to carry a child. Her joy knew no bounds and she was determined to keep the baby at all costs. Nicole was thirty-two when she became pregnant with Brice and given the close bond she had with her mother, she informed her before even telling Brice's father. She didn't know whether he would jump on board but knew her mom would never turn her back on her. Indeed, Brice's father didn't want anything to do with the child and though Nicole was disappointed at first, she was just thankful she had been blessed with a child.

Nicole carried that pregnancy carefully and diligently followed all the instructions the doctors and her mother gave her. She had wished at times her own father was around to witness it but she knew he was watching over her. The pregnancy went well and on that fateful day, she gave birth to a beautiful boy who was named after her father. It was to honor him and to keep his memory alive. Brice David Parker II was his name. He was a beautiful handsome boy. Over the years, Brice had grown into a wonderful boy and, though autistic, he was very talented. Music and art seemed to rule his world and Nicole made sure he had all the resources both in school and at home for him to excel. His birth brought so many blessings to her. She was a flight attendant at the time of his birth and still is but she had also been able to open her own business and was thriving well with it.

Her mother had always been her support, so has her best friend Stephanie. She couldn't ask for another mother like hers and another best friend like Stephanie either. Stephanie made sure to keep food and check on her family every day after the crash. She prayed with her family and made sure they were comfortable. People weren't always this lucky to have amazing people in their lives like this and Nicole counted her blessings. After the birth of Brice, she made a vow not to be involved with anyone else until God blessed her with someone truly deserving.

Nicole was a good young lady who followed God until she met Brice's father. He had promised her so many things but also deceived her. He came into her life as a Christian, a good man who had a head on his shoulders; in the end, she realized he was nothing but a liar and cheat. In her earlier days of pregnancy, she found him with another woman and knew he was a lost cause. From then on, she cut off all communication with him. Being a good person, she did share the birth with him and welcomed him if he wanted to come to visit or be part of his son's life. He never did. Though it worried her for a while, she moved on through the relationship she had now built with her heavenly father.

For the past five years, she had worked to get closer to God and she was so proud of that relationship she had created. Her focus now had been her family, work, and God. She loved to travel and did that often with her son and mother. This past year alone, she was able to take them to Bali, France, and South Africa. Nicole's mom Elena was born and raised in Johannesburg before moving to the United States and married her father Geralt. Her parents would always say it was love at first sight. They met back on campus while her mother was in her junior year and her father in his senior year. They had been like two peas in a pod until her father's demise last year. She wished and hoped for a beautiful story like that. Surely, God had a plan for her as we are reminded in the book of Jeremiah in the Bible. She knows His plans for her will come to pass.

The final check for their arrival was completed by the controller. In about fifteen minutes, they would reach their destination. Nicole checked baby Grace again and she was deeply asleep. In fact, it seemed like she had spent most of the time on the train sleeping. Nicole recalled those times when Brice would also sleep more than anything. How they grew up so fast!

A few minutes later, they arrived and headed out to the waiting area. Nicole spotted her mother and son, immediately. Of course, Stephanie was with them. Brice ran as fast as he could to reach his mom and gave her the best hug anyone could give. She held on to him for a long while before embracing her mom and best friend. Brice was surprised by his mom carrying a baby in a stroller, but he wouldn't bother his mind right now. He just wanted to touch the baby and play with her. He held her hands and gave her the warmest kisses ever when his mom showed her to everyone. She then quickly filled them in about baby Grace. They all felt sad for her but at the same time, they felt happy that Nicole was able to fill in as an adoptive mom until the investigation regarding the crash was completed. No one knew yet who Grace's mom and dad were or if she had a relative, but they believed all would be well with her.

Twenty Five

A part of Keyanna was losing hope, hope that Jules would never be found. At the rate things were going, there wasn't much to uncover and the worst part of it was that none of the passengers found were alive. This was troubling and frightening, and although she had been keeping face, deep down she was terrified. She couldn't fathom living a day without her husband. Jules was her essence of life, her partner, and the one who saw her when she was invisible to the world. Jules had seen her through trying times and loved her with everything in him. Most men in this world would never support and love a girl who was carrying another child from another man.

She could recall how she met Jules. It was at a grocery store. She went that day to get buy food for herself and Kyara. Though she was pregnant, she wasn't showing yet. She was still on campus and was finishing her semester before moving out of the dorms. Since Eric left that semester, she had kept her mind on her studies and for her baby only. She wasn't always herself those days. So when she knocked Jules off balance and he dropped his groceries, she didn't realize it at first. It took a minute for her to come out of her daydream to notice. She quickly helped him pick up the items and, while looking up, their eyes locked. They stared at each other for a long time before getting up on their feet and greeting each other. Of course, Keyanna offered an apology and cleared the air. They talked a bit more that day and even shared their contact information.

Keyanna didn't think anything out of it because she saw it wasn't an opportunity to make a new friend. Little did she know that Jules saw it differently. The next day, he called her and invited her to lunch. She didn't see any harm in that. Back then, she saw everyone as a good person and believed they had good intentions. Though she had become a bit bitter from the way her parents abandoned her with the baby, she didn't latch out on anyone but God through her prayers. She would find herself praying, mumbling all the time, and questioning God for the mess she had found herself in. Though she didn't feel like going out that day, she agreed to it and he came to pick her up later.

Their first date was at a little cafe near her university. It was local but had amazing food. If her mind was right, it was called Joe's. The owner was a friendly African-American man who ran the business with his wife. She loved that place and their turkey and avocado sandwich was to die for. She was thankful Jules took her there that day. They both ordered their food and enjoyed it very much. They talked for hours about everything and anything until she felt sick. That sickness opened the doors to what is today. It changed everything that day.

At this time of her pregnancy, she experienced morning sickness during the day or at night. She didn't know why her morning sickness was different from what most women experienced. So her favorite sandwich turned out to be her worst. She had to throw up and was feeling nauseous. Jules helped her to the bathroom and stood outside until she was done. He then brought her back to her house and asked to stay with her until she felt better. Though he was a stranger then, there was something about him that made her trust him. He stayed and watched over Keyanna till late at night.

"Pregnancy is kicking my butt," said Keyanna when she finally woke up. "I am sorry I had to ruin your day with all of this."

"No worries at all, Keyanna, I'm glad I was able to help you. I didn't know you were pregnant," said Jules. "Congratulations!"

"Thank you. It's a bittersweet situation but I am thankful for it all."

Jules nodded and didn't ask any more questions. Rather he excused himself and left and thanked her for the date. She also thanked him and went back to bed. While in bed, she wondered if she had scared him off as a friend. He seemed like a decent guy and friendly, too. She could use a new friend right now. She loved her best friend but also wanted to have other good friends. She hoped he would overcome the news of her pregnancy and keep in touch.

Though Keyanna felt the beginning of a great friendship was over, she had hope. Her hope sure was alive, for Jules called to check up on her again the next day. After that, their friendship grew. He would help her with her studies and vice versa. When it was time to move off-campus, he offered his assistance and even brought some friends to help that day. They quickly became close and shared more as time went by. Jules was finishing his senior year majoring in biology and planned on going to medical school after that. With time, Keyanna shared her predicament with him about her parents not accepting the pregnancy. He was moved and hurt by what she said.

"How could your parents turn their backs on you this way?" he asked.

"Well, my father has a very important role in our church and because of that, my mom has always been one who wants to keep up with appearances and she worries so much about what others think. She said that tongues will waggle and I was a disappointment. She went as far as asking me to abort the child and told me that once I get married, later on, I could have more children. That's when I acknowledged my mother had lost her way," Keyanna confided in him.

She didn't know the cause but she prayed and hoped that things would one day turn around. And they did. Today, Keyanna's mom is the loving woman she once knew; she loved her grandchildren and spent every day asking for her daughter's forgiveness. She admitted a year after Keyanna had given birth to Sophie that she had wronged her child beyond repair.

If not for Angel, Kyara's mother, Keyanna would have endured even more hardship than she could imagine. Keyanna's saving grace during her pregnancy was for sure Angel, a woman who went above and beyond to support her and Sophie. She was forever grateful to her and now she had given her a place in her heart as her "second" mom. Thinking all of this brought tears to Keyanna's face. Going down memory lane sure was good, but it tended to bring back feelings that were buried or those that she thought had healed.

She told herself: *I have to keep my head up and trust that Jules will be found and the will of God will be done.*

Twenty Six

Caleb could see that Keyanna was more worried as the days went by. He was thankful that she found the other part of the plane. These past days, they were able to recover almost all of the remaining passengers. They had accounted for all except one. That one was Jules. Where could he be? The search had spread out twenty miles, making the crew go around almost the entire island. The only place left was the ocean. Though the plane landed half in-between the land and the sea, he doubted anyone could have been thrown into the ocean by the crash, heavy winds, and rain that occurred that fateful day.

He didn't have the courage to tell Keyanna that the search was closing down. They had been ordered to wrap it up. Though the airline promised to look into the sea, that would take a couple of days to happen. As we know, the ocean tends to spit out anything that doesn't belong in it over time. If there were any bodies in that seawater, they would, for sure, come to the surface. But how would they know? The search team was asked to stay for one more week and, after that, everything would be closed.

Though this might be one of the most challenging things he had done in years, Caleb summoned the courage and went to talk with

Keyanna. As expected, Keyanna was at a loss for words. She was pacing back and forth in her tent with one hand on her chin. The atmosphere got quiet for a long time, then she spoke.

"I know my husband isn't dead. Call it a gut feeling, intuition, or just God telling me he isn't dead. I don't know what's going on but I do know if he is out there, then the God that I serve will watch over him and bring him back to us. I know you are working on rules, policies, and procedures. I won't be a hindrance to that. I do want to look around the island one more time. If I still don't see my husband, then I will need your team to find a way for me to get home." She then walked around the island and didn't come back till nightfall.

Keyanna took that time and went to a secluded place to pray, sing, and call on God. Although her faith was shaky at this moment and her mind was constantly at war with her spirit. One minute, she was questioning God, the next she was praising Him and holding onto hope. It's as if she was fighting an unknown war in her heart, mind, and soul. She had learned one thing over the years: When confusion sets in, just pray, ask for clarity, ask for Him to remind you of his presence. So she did.

"Jehovah God, my Provider, my everything, I thank you for my life today and that of those that I love. Once again, I come to you because I need your help, Father. My world is getting darker and I feel like all the walls are closing in on me. Will you please give me a sign to tell me that my husband is alive? I need that to hold onto this belief in my heart that he is alive. If he is indeed alive, please protect him, cover him with your blood, and bring him back to us in your own time. I have no control over this anymore, so I am leaving it in your hands and letting your will be done in this situation. In Jesus' mighty name I pray. Amen."

Just like that, Keyanna had left this process finally in her Creator's hands. He was the one who had never failed her before. Though she may not have understood the lessons and what God was doing through all this, she somewhat believed it would all be for their good at some point. One day, she would look back and smile and thank God that she overcame this season, too.

The next day, as promised, Caleb rallied the team and they spent nearly all day covering the entire island. Still, there was no sign of Jules. Keyanna felt devastated inside, but she pretended as if she wasn't. She told herself she needed to be strong. That was something that she loved telling herself.

"It's one thing to be strong, but it's another to grieve, Keyanna," said the voice.

She ignored it and prepared herself to go home the next day. The day had been exhausting and draining. She barely ate her soup before sleep crept in. For once, she had fallen asleep since this incident without any trouble.

The next day, Keyanna arose early and was ready to leave the island. Caleb made sure everything was ready for her. She was going to be taken directly to Omaha. The company had arranged that to avoid commercial traveling and seeing the media. Currently, they were everywhere ever since they heard Keyanna and Nicole may be the only survivors. Caleb was thankful right now that no one knew about baby Grace and he intended to keep it that way till further notice. Caleb made sure Keyanna had his contact information as well and prepared them for departure.

The pilot in charge of the flight was a friend of Caleb's and Caleb trusted him with his life. So Caleb knew Keyanna was in good hands and the pilot would do everything to make sure they landed safely. There were other crew members on board. They would be taking the rest of the bodies to Texas for more investigation after Keyanna was dropped off. The pilot would be returning home in a couple of days after the sea search was over. The plane took off smoothly and Caleb stared at it as a little kid watching a plane for the first time. He was thankful that the ocean shore could land the small plane for all this research.

This whole incident brought some darkness back into Caleb's life, too. Seeing all these bodies, Caleb couldn't help but remember his father. Caleb was an only child of Charlotte and Paul Tate. They were loving parents who moved mountains for him to be everything and more. Though he quickly learned at a younger age that he was dyslexic, that never stopped him. His parents gave him the best of the best in education and life in general.

How he missed his father. He was a pilot who served in the Air Force for almost three decades. He had joined fresh out of high school and spent his entire career doing what he loved: flying. Caleb got his love of planes from his father who would give him a small toy plane each Christmas to add to the large collection he already had.

Being an only child and son, he had the chance to create many memories with his dad that were so precious to him. Now, though he was dead, Caleb held on to those memories as the best gifts he had left of him. He lost him nearly five years ago. He had died a natural death and left his mom devastated.

Nevertheless, Caleb made sure he was there for his mother and they had been managing one day at a time. So he may not know what it was to lose a spouse, but he was familiar with the pain of losing someone. He still didn't know how he overcame that grief because his father was also his best friend. It took him a while to come out of his shell again and live a normal life. Despite that, from time to time, he couldn't help but wonder how things would have been if he were still alive. They had so many plans that they were going to do and now he didn't even have the will to do those things.

His mother had become a fragile woman who spent time at home rather than in the company of her elite friends. Caleb's mother came from a prestigious family in the Carolinas. As those would say, she came from old money, so she was used to a fancy lifestyle and so much more in her entire life. That quickly changed when she lost her spouse. It's as if the world had shattered around her. Caleb prayed daily that his mother would one day get back to being herself and have meaning in her life. He, on the other hand, was now thinking more toward starting a family because he felt it was the right time.

Twenty Seven

The plane landed well and safely. Keyanna gathered her things and headed toward the pick-up side. She shared her arrival with her family and they all were excited to see her. She couldn't wait to see her children. She had missed them so much. Upon arriving at the pick-up side of the airline, she saw a huge crowd and some were holding "Welcome Home" signs. She couldn't believe it. She ran toward them with tears in her eyes; so did her children all at the same time. They held each other for a long period of time. She kissed them all over and just enjoyed this moment, this time. It was a priceless moment she almost lost. Janis wanted to be picked up and the girls held each of her hands. She managed her way to embrace her parents and was shocked to see Eric as well.

She looked surprised but still hugged him and found her way to Jules's father. He looked pale and more worried close-up. She hugged him for so long and their eyes spoke more words than their mouths could utter. He knew that the hope of finding his son was slimmer as days went by, but he was hopeful that anything could happen. Keyanna held on to that hope herself.

At home, big soul food meals were set on the table and everyone ushered her to freshen up and join them. Once she settled in at the table, her father took the stage and offered a thank you prayer, acknowledging God for his faithfulness, while also asking Him to bring Jules back to them. Once more, he also asked God for His will to be done. Keyanna thanked all of them for setting up this homecoming feast for her.

"We know this is hard for you, Keke, but we have to be grateful that you are here. We rely on our faith that Jules will come to us soon, too," Keyanna's mother spoke.

Though her kids were around the adults, the family was doing everything they could to not alarm them of their father's situation.

Of course, there would be time for that, just not now. She was happy for the home meals but didn't have much of an appetite. She ate some food and then decided to lay down on the sofa with her children around her. The family cleaned up and Kyara joined her best friend in the living room where they talked at length. Keyanna was at peace telling her friend (turned sister) about her recent experience. She hadn't shared her fears and some of her sentiments till today. Kyara comforted her to the best of her abilities and asked her to be hopeful and to believe he would be found.

I cannot survive without Jules. How can I cope without him? she thought to herself.

Kyara reminded her of her children's presence with a quick sign so she wouldn't cry in front of them. She nodded and quickly wiped her tears. Her friend got up and hugged her from the back of the sofa and spoke encouraging words into her ears. Kyara ushered Keyanna to keep her head up, to stay prayerful, and to know that there was an entire village of support behind her. Indeed, she had this whole family around her: Kyara's mom, Jules's family, her own family, and Eric. She counted herself blessed. Given she was tired and had experienced hard moments these past days, the family left her to retire and rest. They created a rotating schedule where a person would come and help her with the kids, drop meals off for them, and make sure she and the children were fine. She didn't want the help but her mom reminded her that it wasn't her choice to make. She simply nodded and refused to fuss over that with her mom.

The family hugged Keyanna and said their goodbyes. They wanted to give her time to settle in and bond with her children. Taking a look at her children, Keyanna felt overwhelmed. She loved them with all her heartstrings and she wanted them to have both parents in their lives; that's why she was praying constantly in her heart for her husband to be found and to be found alive and safe. She spent the next hours with the kids watching their favorite shows. She then bathed them and put them to bed. How she missed this simple routine. These past days with the plane crash, the days on the island had changed her perspective so much more. She used to love every minute and aspect of her life; she now does even more.

Once the kids settled in, she placed a call to Nicole to check on her and baby Grace. They spent the next hour catching up on the phone and just filling each other in with their own news. She could sense Nicole's happiness in her voice. She was elated for her new friend. She just wished that type of happiness could fill her as well. A couple minutes later, Keyanna found herself holding her husband's picture after the call. She simply missed him. His absence in the house was felt: the way he would walk on tiptoes when the kids were asleep to him welcoming them home after school. Those old memories were playing like a jigsaw puzzle in her mind. She wanted to fill them all, yet release them, too, for they were giving her both happiness and pain at the same time.

She tried to get rid of her husband's memories in her head, but they kept getting stronger and stronger. She screamed so loudly that Janis's cries brought her back. She ran to check on her son and rocked him back to sleep. Slowly walking back to the living room, where she had found comfort in the sofa, Keyanna wondered what had just happened to her. She held on tightly to the pillows and decided to wear one of her husband's shirts before falling asleep. That soothed her and gave her some sort of peace for the night. The night surely was long for her. She tossed and turned a while before finally resting.

Despite falling asleep late, she still woke up a couple of times to check on the kids. Having a ranch-style home made access to the children's rooms easy for her. They were all on the same level which made it easy for Keyanna to check on her kids a couple of times through the night. It was one of the reasons they chose this house design when they were searching for a new home. She loved this home. Though it was a ranch, they added a basement addition to it and a room that was reserved for guests. Most of the time, she would stay there when her best friend came over to spend ladies' night with her. This house held so many memories and she prayed she could create more.

Twenty Eight

Sophie had always been an early riser since her childhood times. She would be up at the crack of dawn and spend hours in her room playing with her dolls, toys, and anything that she considered fun. She still had that spirit in her. Once up, she had found her way slowly into her mom's bed and snuggled right under her arms.

This time, Sophie found her mother on the sofa. Keyanna felt a presence and shifted her body closer to the back of the sofa so they would not fall. She slightly gave Sophie a kiss on her head and then held her tightly close to her body. She could feel her warmth and it was good as always. These were some of the priceless moments that she wouldn't trade in motherhood. Being loved unconditionally was the best gift ever. They stayed snuggling until Janis and his sister came along as well.

Keyanna knew the party was over when they all jumped on her, kissed her, and wanted to be held all together. She greeted and kissed them all.

"Good morning!" she said.

Of course, Janis asked for Daddy. She reminded them that he was on a trip and would be back soon. They showed their disappointing faces but got over it again once they heard Keyanna ask them what they wanted for breakfast. That always got them excited. They wanted pancakes, waffles, and no cereal. Everyone had their own suggestions.

Keyanna then said, "Let's make pancakes together, guys." They all agreed.

Whatever she said, most days was a yes. For them, they were always happy as long as it was their mom doing it. She helped them brush their teeth and bathe them; they helped her make the pancakes in their own ways. It was more of chaos than help, but she was grateful and happy they were part of the process. She strived to change certain things she experienced while growing up. She wanted to create memories with her kids and she believed in discipline without trauma. Parenting wasn't always easy, but she believed with learning, accepting constructive criticism, and praying, her husband and she would surely do right by their children. So, in turn, they could be good for society and fulfill the purposes God had called them to accomplish.

Once breakfast was finished, Keyanna cleaned herself up and reached out to her employer. In her absence, her parents had taken the initiative to inform them of the accident. They had given her a week off until further notice. However, with everything going on, she wanted to take a family leave of absence. She needed time for clarity and Jules needed her should he return home. She wanted to be there and be ready to make sure he would have the support of his family.

She took her phone and placed a call to her manager. Though Keyanna worked for this particular company, she also had a small consulting business. She had contracts with small business owners and offered services: bookkeeping, preparing taxes, and fulfilling other financial needs. Once she was connected to her manager, she shared her news with her and asked for more time off. They then talked for a while before disconnecting. Keyanna needed to reach back to Human Resources to fill out all the paperwork for family leave of absence. This particular moment definitely wasn't the time for her to work for anyone. Thankfully, on her small business side, she had Kyara as an assistant from time to time and Kyara had been keeping up with her clients' needs ever since the crash occurred.

Getting back to the kids, she stood in the distance watching them as they played and ran around the house. She surely was counting her blessings and thanking God for each and every one of them. She hadn't heard anything from the investigation crew about the crash site yet, but she continued to believe that Jules was alive. The doorbell ring brought her attention back. It must have been the food delivery her mom had told her about yesterday. Though she wasn't up for all of that, she recalled the calendar, and given it was almost eleven, she figured it would be one of them. She quickly opened the door and as she imagined, it was Kyara. They hugged for a long time before Kyara settled into the house and made sure all the food and drinks were stored in their right places.

The good friends spent hours talking and just remembering all they had gone through in their own paths and how God had always kept them together. Kyara worried a bit for Keyanna because she wasn't herself. Though Kyara could see that her best friend was trying hard to keep it together, she knew Keyanna was hurting a whole lot. Kyara managed to stay away from the topic but really wanted to check in. So she took her best friend downstairs where the kids would be away from them.

Then she asked, "How are you holding up, Sis? I know you and I can tell you are doing your best to keep your spirits up but it's not working. I want to check in with you. Talk to me."

The next thing that came out were tears, heavy ones with screaming and Kyara reached out and held Keyanna in her arms.

"Let it all out, Sis, I got you," Kyara reminded her.

She hugged Keyanna and kept her close to her for quite some time before letting her go.

Kyara said, "You needed that and I am glad I was here for you. I want you to start journaling again. For now, Keyanna, just write your daily thoughts down. You know we love self-therapy, and in a situation like this, as your sister, I want you to start practicing it. I believe it will help you until you are ready to see an actual therapist. You know in this house and mine, God and therapy go hand in hand."

Keyanna nodded and thanked her friend.

"To be honest, Kyara, I don't want to believe that Jules is dead. Though his body hasn't been found yet, a part of me still believes he is alive. If I can just figure out where, I would go and rescue him myself," Keyanna managed to say.

Kyara reminded her, "Keyanna, that's what the authorities are for. I am sure the rescue team is doing all they can to find him. I know they have recovered everyone but him, but there is hope and we have to hold on to it. In the meantime though, Jules would want you to be strong and present for the kids, so please try and hold it together for them. I believe Jules will return to you all soon."

She hugged her friend one more time and then left for the day. She reminded Keyanna that another person would come in the evening with their meals as the schedule showed.

Keyanna admitted that these meal deliveries were good for them. She wasn't much in the state of cooking again so she was grateful.

Twenty Nine

Caleb was exhausted from the search. Though the island was nearly empty, he was still there with some of his crew. He joined this part of the job after being a pilot for a few years with the company. Though becoming a pilot was his dream, he felt like something was missing and he needed a better purpose. So he switched his position to the search unit manager a couple of months ago. He loved it because he was often a bearer of good news (well, sometimes bad). When a plane crashes, it is never a good thing but having the resources to search and find the passengers and bring them back to their families gave him a purpose. After all, someone had to do it.

He didn't know why he had switched jobs; he just knew that after the death of his father who was also a pilot, he needed a change. Regardless, this particular crash had crushed his spirit. He had never experienced a crash like this before. A lot of people had lost their lives and they were still searching for one person he didn't think would ever be found. How could he bear this news to anyone? Anyone, especially Keyanna. She seemed like a wonderful soul and he felt like this would break her. The diving team had searched for the past two days and there were no bodies to be found. They even did another round of the island with no results. He had officially received word from a higher level to conclude all searches.

Though another crew would come and take the plane parts for further investigation, he wanted to wait for that crew and make sure there was no one left under the remaining parts. It's been a week already and if there were any bodies in the sea, they would have surfaced on the shore by now. Throughout the search, they did find a cave with a couple who claimed to be living on the island for years now. They commuted via their boat to the mainland for things they needed. Caleb was amazed how they lived here all alone, but he also thought that it would be a fun experience to do someday in his lifetime.

Caleb was worried. He talked with his crew and the cleanup began. He was also in charge of notifying Keyanna and Nicole about the news. The boarding pass list showed no infant's name registered for boarding. No one knew who the parents were. The airline planned to share that with the authorities and send baby Grace to social services. Caleb really hoped a wonderful family would be able to take care of the baby.

Caleb placed his first call to Nicole and shared the news with her. She was devastated but also curious to know how the baby got on board. She told Caleb something he wasn't ready for.

"I'm a licensed foster parent, so I will go to the headquarters to talk with social services and present myself as a potential foster parent. Brice has fallen in love with baby Grace and so have we all. I don't want to let her go. I want to foster her and, if possible, one day adopt her.

Caleb stayed mute for a while before speaking.

"That's amazing, Nicole. I am sure Grace will be overjoyed. I was just praying and wishing that she would be connected to a great family. I hope it all works out for you, Nicole. You have my number, so please call me if you need anything. I will let the management know that they should be expecting you and Grace."

"Thank you, Caleb, I truly appreciate your help and effort in this search. Give Keyanna my love and I will be calling her also to check on her because she is going to need lots of support after you give her the news," Nicole explained.

Both colleagues said their goodbyes and Caleb proceeded to call Keyanna.

Upon seeing the caller ID, Keyanna's heart skipped for a minute. This call could change so many things in her life. At first, she didn't want to pick it up, so she rang her voicemail. She then noticed Caleb didn't leave a voicemail message. Then right then, Caleb tried again. This time, she picked up and greeted him.

"How are you holding up?" asked Caleb.

"Oh, I have had better days but I am alive."

Caleb could hear the sadness in Keyanna's voice. She was good at being strong but, just like everyone, she was hurting, and here he was about to add to that load.

Caleb talked next. "Keyanna, we had the team of divers do their own search and, unfortunately, we still didn't find any bodies. Your husband's body, based on our prediction, would have surfaced if truly he was in that water by now. Then again, that's science for you. I am hopeful that heaven can do more than that and God always has the last say. I am sorry to be the bearer of bad news."

Caleb took a deep breath and continued. "The airline has decided to stop the searches for now. The next step is to have another crew clean up the plane's pieces and the island. That will take weeks if not months to be done. Anything can happen. I know this is hard for you because if his body was found, at least it would have given you and your family some closure. But sadly, we don't have that yet. Though I will leave the island, I will still be in contact with the new crew and will keep you informed as things unravel. I will be sending details and contact information to you with our loss team. Per our guidelines and rules, they have to work with you to create a compensation package for your loss. The airline will be compensating the families of those who lost their lives and also offer a memorial service for them."

Keyanna listened as Caleb shared more information. "I know Jules is missing and that a service may not be something your family wants to do yet, so you are not obligated to attend. I do hope you will be open to the compensation because it will be something helpful for your children in the long run. Keyanna, please don't hesitate to call me anytime you wish to talk or have any questions. I am here for you. Nicole promised to be there for you as well and I pray and hope so will your family. You are not alone."

Keyanna could barely breathe. She slowly found herself searching for a seat as she was standing earlier when the call came through.

Her throat was so tight, she couldn't find herself letting any words out. She also suddenly felt like she was suffocating and all the air in the world couldn't be enough for her. She didn't recall the last thing she said or when the phone got disconnected.

At that particular moment, she felt like a moving truck had just hit her, dragged her through the ground, and now she was left in a deep hole that she couldn't crawl out of. A new feeling crept slowly inside of her heart. *How can this be? We were just getting each other back and had many years of living and enjoying life. What kind of game is the universe playing with me? My husband is gone? No, that can't be. Jules can never leave me. He never left me during my pregnancy, even when the child I was bearing wasn't his, so why now?*

Now that they had overcome that pregnancy, gotten married, and built a family, he was gone. Jesus, have mercy! I cannot bear this. What do I tell my children? How do I cope? I know I am resilient but not to this extent.

Keyanna's mind raced with so many thoughts and it didn't find any answers to her questions. Rather, she sank deep, deep into a state of denial that no one could get her out of. She slowly crawled under the sheets on the sofa and found herself weeping. She was weeping so hard that Sophie, who had just woken up from a nap, ran to her wondering what was wrong. Keyanna quickly turned on her mommy's face and told her child that everything was okay. However, her mind still wondered how she could cope and do this. She wasn't prepared for this. Life was truly unfair to take her husband from her.

She refused to believe he was dead, but she lost hope in finding him, for it would probably be impossible. At this moment, she, the one who was always hopeful and trusted God in everything, had somehow let go of that belief. "Where is God in all of this?" she asked out loud.

While she rocked Sophie, another food delivery came. The doorbell rang again. *Who could it be this time?* she wondered. Slowly, Sophie and she got to the door and opened it. To her shock, it was Eric.

Keyanna's mother had mentioned the meal deliveries, but she never asked who would be delivering them.

"Eric?" she asked in surprise.

"Well, hello to you, too. How are you holding up?" he asked.

"Why is everyone asking me that?" she snapped.

"I'm sorry, Keyanna. It wasn't my intention to make you angry. I'm just worried about you just like everyone else."

"That's easy for you to say. How can someone who abandoned me with a pregnancy tell me he is worried about me? You left me with no explanation just after I had given my pride to you."

What?!" Jules exclaimed.

Keyanna realized she just dropped a bomb and she wasn't supposed to do that. Sophie was also still holding her hands.

Keyanna looked down at Sophie, "Hi sweety, can you please go play with your sister and brother?" She shook her head and ran toward the playroom where her siblings were.

Eric quietly put the meals on the kitchen counter where he had walked to. Keyanna followed him and apologized for going off on him.

"I am sorry, Eric. I just received a call I wasn't expecting and it really shook me off my balance."

"What was the call about," he asked.

"Well, it was the airline company telling me about how they were closing the search. Jules still hasn't been found and they aren't declaring him missing, but somewhat dead. To be honest, I don't think I heard the rest of what the guy said."

"I am so sorry, Keyanna. Should I call everyone so they can come over tonight?"

"No, don't. I want to be alone tonight. Maybe you can help me tell them to come in the morning for a family meeting so we could talk?"

"Of course, consider that done."

"Thanks also for bringing the food. You can let yourself out, Eric. I am sorry but I am not in my right sense of mind to talk right now. I appreciate you stopping by though." She then walked off and headed toward her bedroom.

That evening, Keyanna didn't find herself doing much with her kids, rather she fell into a state of even more denial. She made sure she fed her children and read books to them. She was happy that they were on spring break and didn't have school this week. She didn't know what all of that would look like when they returned to school. For now, this day was over and they were all tucked in bed. She was also in her bed and found herself looking at Jules's side of the bed from time to time. Though she fought with the pain and turned and tossed for a while, she eventually caught some sleep.

Thirty

Eric could barely walk to his door. *What in the world did Keyanna just say?* He was overwhelmed. Once in his car, he took time to just race things through his mind.

It was not possible that Keyanna got pregnant back then and never told me anything. Could she be right or was it just her grief speaking rubbish? He asked himself millions of questions, replayed scenarios in his head to remember those days in college, but still couldn't come up with any answers. He knew the people who would be able to answer so he headed their way. One of them would surely spill the truth. He wasn't going to sit and wait on this. *A child?* The same child his ex-wife couldn't have because she was too focused on her career and didn't want any children to slow her down. Now there was a chance…he had one all along. Heck, he would find out tonight.

He found himself driving so fast and the road was so long, even though Kyara's house was barely a ten-minute drive from Keyanna's. When he got there, he went into the house as if he lived there. Kyara's kids were still playing outside and the door was open.

Kyara shouted, "What is your problem? Is someone after you or did you see a ghost?"

"I didn't see any ghosts and no one was after me. I just experienced something crazy now at Keyanna's."

"And what is that, if I may ask?"

"Well, she told me I abandoned a pregnancy and left her hanging. And so I have no right to say that I am worried about her."

"Is that why you ran into my house like that? Well, I am sorry to be the bad news bearer, but you did leave a pregnancy on her head. I know this isn't the right way for you to find out but I knew sooner or later this would happen."

Eric almost dropped to his knees. He had to quickly sit at one of the kitchen island chairs so he wouldn't lose his balance. It felt like his worst nightmare was right in front of him and he would soon wake up from it.

"How can Keke do this to me?" he asked.

"First of all, she is no longer your Keke and you did that to yourself, sir. You are the one who broke up things without even telling her why. Then you got up and moved to an unknown destination with no contact number left behind."

"I know what I did then was bad, but I don't deserve this. I should have known about my child."

"Eric, first of all, she is not your child. And second, this is definitely not the time to cause any problems for Keke. She is grieving, confused, and going through a lot right now. I will advise you to cool off for now and give it time."

"I know but…," said Eric.

"Okay, I shouldn't have even confirmed this to you but I believe it's time you know the truth given you are back in town anyway. You know how people talk around here, so sooner or later someone would say it to your face."

"So everyone knows except me?"

"Of course," replied Kyara. "Are you that blind, Eric? Can't you see Keyanna's first child is a spitting image of your mother?"

"I noticed that the last time I saw her at Keke's party but I thought I was crazy."

"Well, you aren't. Anyway, how is Keke?"

"She isn't doing well. And with the phone call she claimed she had received earlier before my visit, she is in a state of mind I have never seen her in."

Kyara quickly picked up her phone and called Keke. She tried many times but there was no answer. Eric reminded her that Keyanna had asked for time alone and wanted all of the family to meet at her house tomorrow morning. Though Kyara was worried for her friend, she believed in giving her the space she needed to process everything that happened. So Eric and Kyara informed the family about being at Keyanna's house in the morning.

Once that was done, Eric left for his own place. Eric wasn't a local in Omaha. He visited when he could for his father; some family was still around but this time, he had decided to stay. He moved back a month ago and was still settling in. He was tired of traveling and thought he had done enough of that and wanted to settle in one place again. He bought a townhome before arriving and had it all furnished to his taste. He had worked hard all his life and loved living in luxury. He was always that guy who drove the nicest car and wore the nicest clothes. He loved the attention and also knew he was good-looking. Keyanna never liked that part of him and used to always put him in check when they were together.

Even though he promised to let go of this subject, for now, he couldn't help but wonder why. He agreed to have wronged Keyanna and treated her badly, but he didn't deserve to be put in the dark like he was. To think that almost everyone knew but him. So his dad may be aware of this also? He refused to believe that but he would, for sure, check that tomorrow. Eric couldn't help but think of the possibilities and the path that life could have given them. He was stupid back in those college days and regretted every day what he had done to Keke. He had always wondered how he could make it up to her but he was too afraid to come around and tell her that.

Things got even worse when he found out she was married and moved back to Omaha to be closer to her parents. He knew then that he had lost her forever. He loved her, heck he still did. He just had to learn not to show that side because he feared what would result. He went on to get married, too, so he could fill that void Keyanna left in him. A year later, he realized both he and his ex were married for the wrong reasons so they both decided to walk away peacefully. He was thankful a child didn't come out of their marriage because it would have been another mistake. The child would have been a blessing but now, they would be raising a child in two households. God had always had his back and he was thankful for that. Eric had learned this lesson quickly before things got out of control.

The night was hard for Eric as well. He woke up a couple of times with nightmares that he couldn't understand. He found himself praying and falling back asleep afterward. The next day, he was up at the crack of dawn and decided to hit the gym to burn off all these things that were racing in his mind. After the gym, he freshened up and headed to Keyanna's for the family meeting. Given their past, Keyanna's family still considered Eric as part of their family. Eric's mother and Keyanna's mom were the best of friends. They grew up together and were very close before she passed away. So regardless of their children's history, Mrs. LeFevre could never turn her back on Eric when he came to town. She was aware of his return before anyone else and was glad.

It was close to eleven in the morning when everyone gathered in Keyanna's home. There were her parents, Eric's dad, Jules's father, and a distant uncle as well as Kyara, her children, and her husband. Kyara thought it would be good for the children to come so they could play with Sophie and her siblings. In fact, she was right. Her children didn't make it to the door before they all hugged and ran toward the playroom. She had to remind them to wash their hands before anything else. They sure did in a hurry and off they went!

Everyone greeted each other and waited for Keyanna to share the news. All of a sudden, the room got quieter. Keyanna saw Eric but acted as if he wasn't there. She had too much on her plate to worry about Eric and what she said yesterday. A part of her mind knew that the topic would be revisited again but, for now, she didn't care. She welcomed everyone once she saw that they settled in. Thanks for honoring this meeting. I pray we can think through this and know what the next steps will be.

Yesterday, I received a call from the airline company announcing that Jules's body was never found. They are closing the search because they believe everything has been done. The agent went further to share that the plane debris will be cleaned up in the months to come and if anything happens between now and then, they would let us know. As she spoke, her face roamed the room and she saw the way everyone took the news. They all were hit by it one way or the other. Disappointment and a feeling of hopelessness fell on their faces as well. The room got quieter, worse than before. Then someone spoke.

"I am sorry we are going through this, Keyanna," said Jules's father. "I love my son and would have wished I had a chance to say goodbye. But all the same, I thank God for everything. I can't seem to understand why things happen this way or what the message is, but I do know God has a reason for all of this. It doesn't make sense now and it hurts badly. But I am here for you and the kids and I hope you will be for me, too." Beau had spoken as a true elder like he was. Keyanna walked over to him and gave him a lasting hug.

The rest of the family hugged Keyanna and spoke comforting words to her. They also asked her if she was willing to do a service for her husband and they told her they were ready to help her whenever she was. They could continue to bring meals to Keyanna and her children for as long as she wanted. They volunteered to drop off and pick up the kids from school to help alleviate her needs. Talking with her mom, later on, Keyanna had enlisted her help to contact the airline company and help sort out those things for her. As for Kyara, she would be in charge of helping her with her family leave.

Keyanna wasn't ready to do any service for her husband. Her heart wasn't there yet. When it was time, she would inform the others. For now, she was thankful for them and all the help they offered. Everyone noticed that Keyanna tried to be outwardly her best but one person who knew it was worse than what it seemed like was Kyara. So Kyara decided to stay the night and asked her husband to look after the kids. She simply told him that she needed to be with Keyanna because Keyanna needed her. Before departing, Beau prayed with Keyanna and the family and they all gave her love.

Thirty One

Indeed, Keyanna needed help. She could barely bathe the kids that evening. Thank God for her friend (turned sister). Kyara made sure the kids were fed, bathed, and played with before kissing them goodnight. She also prayed with them and read them one of their favorite stories. Once the kids were in bed, she joined her best friend who was also lying in bed. She snuggled up next to her and they both stayed there in silence for hours. Then Kyara got tired.

"Keke, you can't go on like this. I know I don't completely understand what you are going through, but I do know you are strong and you can overcome this. I need you to get back to that, girl! I know who was pushed down years back but never let it be her final fall!"

"I just want my husband, Kyara."

"I know you do, Keke, and you are going to want him for a long time because he was part of you. But I want you to know that he isn't here now and you ought to be strong for the children that you both had."

"I don't know how," replied Keyanna.

"Yes, you do. It is there inside of you and I need you to tap into it. Let's do a quick session. I know you aren't in the mood but let's try. If it's too much, I promise I will leave you alone."

Hesitant, Keyanna got up and joined her friend who moved to the floor to be more comfortable. Kyara was a therapist, though she never took Keyanna as a patient. She always helped her friend from time to time when in need.

"Let's begin. Remember, if it gets too much, I want you to tap into your happy place. I know you have one given you have shared with me some of your progress with your own therapist."

Keke nodded.

"Breathe in, breathe out. Let your mind work its own magic. Tell me where you are and we can begin from there. Remember, this is just to release some of the pressure you are building up."

Keyanna inhaled and exhaled for a while and followed her best friend's suggestion. She found herself in the plane when the turbulence started happening.

"Okay, tell me what's going on."

"I'm holding Jules's hand and we are praying, telling each other how much we love each other and that God was going to see us through this turbulence. I also told him that I have completely forgiven him and was glad we made it back to each other. He then kissed my new ring and my hands and told me he was glad and grateful as well."

Keyanna's breathing got so hard that Kyara asked her to come back and go to her happy place.

"Stay with me. I am here with you, Keke. Breathe more and focus on your happy place."

Keyanna stayed there for a while and then slowly came back to her friend. Kyara gave her the warmest hug ever and held her tight.

"How do you feel, Sis?"

"I am exhausted," she replied with tears running down her cheeks.

"You did great. Here is some water. I want you to lay down and just relax. I am proud of you for wanting to try. It will take some time, Keke, but you will get there with God and therapy, remember."

Keyanna smiled at her friend for that was a sentence they always used. "With God and therapy, Kyara," repeated Keyanna before she fell asleep. Kyara tucked her friend in and said a prayer for her before freshening up and hitting the bed herself. While in the shower, she ran the entire situation over in her mind and wondered why this would happen now. Her friend was on the verge of rekindling her marriage with her husband and then this happened. *What kind of an obstacle was this?*

Though in every bad situation, we always believe life is going to end and things won't get better, it surely does. She had seen many times how difficult times have passed to give light to beautiful days. This will surely pass, too. Kyara just hoped it wouldn't break her friend. She made sure she checked on the children before retiring to bed. She slept next to her friend to keep an eye on her through the night.

Beau was dropped off at home by his in-laws. He settled in nicely and wondered why he wasn't given the chance to have his son buried. He was thankful for the life God had granted him but he wished things would have been a bit different in the "burying his children department."

He said to God in a quiet tone, "I wish they would have buried me instead, Father. This pain is hard but I know your plans and I have learned not to doubt them. The person I worry more about is Keyanna. She is a young wife with three children. How will she cope?"

A silent voice replied, *"Trust in the Lord with all your heart."*

Beau simply shook his head and said out loud, "I hear you, Lord. All I ask is for you to help Keyanna through this."

Mr. and Mrs. LeFevre were in shock with the recent news that Keyanna had shared with them earlier. They didn't know what to say and were thankful Beau spoke those true words to Keyanna. Losing a spouse or someone close is something many do not get over so they were worried for their child.

"Keyanna was strong but how much stronger can someone be?" her mom asked. "Father, you have to intervene in this situation. Please heal our daughter's heart and give her comfort as she navigates through this journey. We know you see it all and know it all. Though it may not be to our own understanding, we simply ask for peace over her and the children."

"Amen," replied her husband.

Thirty Two

Everyone was worried for Keyanna and her children. And at this moment, she truly needed her village to be there for her. Kyara saw the turns and struggles her best friend (turned sister) endured through the night. She had a series of nightmares and had woken up quite a few times. Kyara realized this was something bigger than all of them. It sure wasn't bigger than God, so in the middle of the night, she created a group chat where she asked that everyone commit to praying daily for Keyanna's healing and for her overcoming this grief and sadness that had swallowed her up deep. She told them that it was more than what met the eyes. She would connect her best friend to her therapist and also take her to the doctor for a possible sleep remedy. She could easily tell from her sleep habits that her friend was barely sleeping.

Though the next day's morning routine took longer than expected, Kyara and Keyanna made it to the doctor. The doctor was a family doctor who had seen Keyanna before and now her children.

"Sleep deprivation can create many things, especially for someone who has children, Keyanna. I am glad that Kyara brought you in today. I am going to prescribe something that will help you sleep better. Once you realize that you are getting back on your own routine, please stop the pills. I will recommend a follow-up visit in two weeks just to see how things are going," the doctor explained.

"Thank you, Dr. Spencer. We appreciate you," Kyara said.

"Take it easy now, you two."

Both ladies nodded and left for home.

Their children were with Kyara's husband for the day and Kyara had planned to spend the day with her friend. She thought that maybe doing some of the things Keke liked to do would bring her back to herself a bit. So she had booked them time at the spa and also there, they would be getting a pedicure, manicure, and massage. Keyanna, at first, didn't want to go but her sister knew how to convince her easily. They both went and enjoyed their time together. They talked about anything and everything except the accident. Kyara realized that it would take someone else for Keke to open up.

Later that day, when everything was quiet, she reintroduced the idea of therapy to Keyanna.

"I am praying for you and with you, Sis. But I also want you to connect with someone who can help you. I think it's time. I don't want you to wait forever and sink deeper, Keke. Please consider this. As your friend, you know I won't lead you astray."

Keyanna gazed at her for a long time and told her that she would give it a try. She even shocked her friend by telling her that she started journaling this morning again.

Kyara was surprised. "Oh wow! Great, I am happy you did that. It's going to help you. I want you to release all that anger, the feelings, and the sadness in that journal. Don't keep it inside. I know things will get better with time."

Keyanna agreed. "I know they will, too, Kyara. I just feel numb to everything right now."

She has a problem with grief but there might be some slight depression in there, too, Kyara thought. All the same, she was happy Keke has agreed to be on board for therapy. She would connect her to her regular therapist tomorrow. She was also thankful that they were able to solve two problems today.

"You made progress, Keyanna. I am proud of you," her friend said.

Even though Caleb didn't have any reason to reach out to Nicole, he couldn't help it. He wanted to see how she was coping with Grace and her family. He put a call through and got Nicole on the first ring.

"Hi, Caleb! How are you?" Nicole asked.

They exchanged greetings and then he shared his reasons for the call. Nicole was delighted that he cared and was happy to announce to him that she has been approved to be Grace's foster parent for now. Brice and her mom were also so happy for this new addition to the family.

"I'm glad that it all worked out for you, Nicole," Caleb said.

"Thank you, Caleb. You know, I have learned in my short-lived life that our hardest tribulations or troubles usually bring the best blessings ever. Who would have thought that I would gain a beautiful child through all this chaos?"

Caleb sighed and replied, "Yes, you are right. I guess we all have to look at things in a positive way."

They chatted a bit more and Caleb hung up. There was something about her that he just couldn't wrap his mind around. The first time he saw her, he tried so hard to avoid eye contact. She had those eyes that could look into someone's soul and read them on the spot.

Though she wasn't dressed up when they met, he still recalled how he thought she was beautiful. From her complexion to the way she carried herself, the next days before she left the island, Caleb had watched every one of her movements carefully. At one point, he was caught by a colleague for looking at her and daydreaming. There was something really special about her that made him lose his balance and senses anytime she was around. He couldn't pinpoint it but he would someday. Just like now, he could barely say much over the phone because her voice did wonders to him.

A call jolted Caleb back to his phone. It was his mother.

"How are you, old lady?" That was a name he often called his mom to tease her.

"I am well and waiting on you to bring me that lady who will make you settle down."

"You got jokes, mom," replied Caleb. "No, I don't, sweetie. I am just praying hard for you to bring me a nice lady who will bless me with grandkids before my old age."

"Don't worry, God will make a way for me to find that lady sooner or later."

"I am glad you have left that task in His hands. Don't you forget that you must carry it on your shoulder for Him to put it on your head. God will lead you but you still have to do the work for it to work."

"I know and I am willing to do that, Mother," Caleb replied.

Thirty Three

It had been a month since the crash happened. Keyanna's family had been so helpful in assisting her with the meals, the children, and the house chores. Keyanna was finally on family leave and had also done everything that was required of her to get the funds that the airline was paying. She, however, wasn't ready to bury her spouse yet. She still refused to accept that he was dead. She had hoped that there would be more news from Caleb when the crew cleaned the island but nothing came. Caleb only called to check on her and the kids from time to time.

She was still herself, though she had been keeping up with journaling. She hadn't taken the steps to see the therapist as her best friend had suggested. She just did not feel ready. Kyara knew that it was better not to push her. They all just gave her the love she needed, the space she demanded, and the fellowship she might not have asked through the prayer group that Kyara created.

Keyanna felt as if everyone had gone back to their daily lives and she also felt stuck in one place. Today, when she got up, she missed Jules more than ever. She especially missed the jokes he made and how he always kept the house alive with his music. Music, something that was strange to her ears now. She didn't recall the last time she played anything on her phone. The house was quiet. Her children were back in school. She slowly got up from bed and decided to play some music. Her bed was the only place she spent most of her days and time now. It was more comfortable than anything else. She was thankful for her best friend who managed to drag her out of the house now and then, but she still loved her bed more than anything right now.

She picked up Jules's iPad and played the first playlist that showed up. It was a jazz playlist of all his favorites. She also decided to write her thoughts out.

"Dear Jules, today I woke up feeling empty not having you on the side of the bed. I missed your smile, your laugh, your smell. Mostly, I missed you tippy-toeing into the house late at night trying not to wake up the kids, and still Sophie sensed you miles away. (She smiled.) How can it be that I can't see you anymore? I wonder if I will ever see you again, my love. It feels so lonely here. Today, I ask that you give me the strength to go on. I know our kids need it and I am finding it very difficult to do anything. Will you help me? If truly you are gone, which I refuse to accept, lend me a hand. But if you are still alive, I pray for the same strength for you and also that you find your way home soon. I love you, Juju."

She slowly laid back down in her bed and let the music soothe her for the hours to come. Tonight would be a busy one for the kids who were going to a birthday party. She had to keep face and be there. If it were up to her, she wouldn't go but for her children's sake, she would try. They eventually went to the birthday event that evening and she felt a little bit more alive. She was able to play with her kids and be like a child again. That was something she hadn't truly done ever since her husband passed.

Wait a minute! Did I just say passed? she questioned herself. "*So does it mean my spirit is finally agreeing with this? No, it can't be. My husband is not dead.*"

Doing her regular drop-off and check-in on her friend, Kyara came through the house and noticed the door was unlocked. She knew the children were spending the weekend over at their grandparents so she was worried. She rushed in only to find Keyanna on the floor barely breathing. She panicked and started performing CPR and also called 911. The next minutes felt like hours before the paramedics arrived. They rushed Keke to the hospital. Kyara informed her husband and Eric only. She didn't want to put more worry on the elderly that she thought they weren't capable of handling for now.

Kyara followed the ambulance to the ER where Alfred, her husband, and Eric had joined her.

"Do we know anything yet?" asked Eric.

"No, no one came to talk to me yet. I pray she is fine. Let's all hope so," said Alfred.

After about an hour or two, a young doctor came asking for Keyanna's family. They all got up and walked toward her.

"We are her family," they said at once together.

"I'm Dr. Walker and I was the one who received her and treated her so far. We have done some blood work and are waiting on the results but the ones that came through show no sign of infection or anything bad. They are all normal. From my point of view, Keyanna is under a lot of stress and that might be affecting her. I can even say she isn't sleeping well for she looks very pale."

The doctor continued. "Is there something we should know or watch out for? We got her medical history from her primary physician."

Kyara stepped up and filled in the doctor with Keyanna's recent predicament and all that her friend was going through.

He sighed and now understood a bit more about the signs he was seeing. After talking to Kyara, he might be forced to put her on depression medicine and recommend therapy. Kyara told him that she had suggested therapy, too, and also thought Keyanna had started going almost a month ago.

"I don't know if that's the case," said Dr. Walker, "but I will check with her once her final results are in. I will keep you updated."

Once he walked away, they all breathed out a sigh of relief thanking heaven that it wasn't anything serious. Obviously, depression and trauma are bad but, at least, they aren't life-threatening, yet.

"Do you think that?" asked Eric. "Keyanna needs to have someone around 24/7 and therapy needs to be enforced for her. She shouldn't be given a choice anymore."

Kyara laughed a little and asked him if he had forgotten the person they were talking about. This was Keke, the most stubborn person Kyara knew. This was someone who you couldn't nearly force to do anything unless she was willing. Yes, Eric had forgotten that part of her.

"Well, we will try and make sure she gets the help she needs. We owe her that much," Kyara said.

The night was long. Alfred, Kyara, and Eric spent it at Keyanna's bedside. She was going to be released in the morning. The doctor did recommend therapy, prescribed a new sleeping pill for her, and also recommended some vitamins and dietary supplements. She needed to come back to being herself and now it was up to them to help her. This wasn't the Keyanna they all knew.

Thirty Four

Keyanna came home and couldn't remember much, other than passing out when she went to the kitchen to get some water to drink. She was lucky that Kyara had come at that moment. It could have been worse. She realized she was slowly killing herself and needed to come back to reality for her own sake and family, too. Once settled in, Alfred and Eric went on to their daily routine, but Kyara stayed.

"I am sorry that I haven't started therapy as I promised," she mumbled.

"No worries, Keke. I understand you may not have been ready for it."

"Actually, that's not it, Kyara. I know inside my heart, that I have to face my deepest fear and somewhat accept it when I'm in therapy. That's why I don't want to go."

"So what's your deepest fear, Keke, if I may ask?"

She looked the other way for a while and then said, "Accepting that Jules is dead and he may never come back to us."

"Why is that your deepest fear?"

"It's more so to the fact that I never said goodbye. It's also because we were just starting over and recreated another chapter of our lives. I feel like death cheated me on this one. God couldn't have done this to me, to us. I have spent days and nights asking why but the silence is killing me. I can't hear God speaking to me; I can't hear myself speaking to me. I feel lost."

"I'm so sorry you feel that way but grief has so many stages and you are going through all of them. I do believe that you will come out strong and you will be alright. I just want you to give a chance to yourself to heal and find a way to be you again for your children's sake. They miss you and want you. They might not say it as we adults do but they are in need of their parents. Right now, you are both parents and you have to first tell them about their father. I have discussed this with Alfred and I will be staying with you for the next month to help you get back on track. My children will come and stay here and we will use the guest room. You need us and we got you," Kyara suggested.

Keyanna couldn't hold back her tears. She knew it was time for her to try for everyone's sake. So she agreed to start therapy and also prepare herself to talk with her children. The kids would be back tomorrow.

"I want you to try and speak with them," said Kyara.

The rest of the day went well and Keyanna took time to rest. For once in a long time, she took a long nap and was deep asleep. She woke up energized and wanted to eat. More so, she also asked Jules's father to come in the morning and her parents, too. She wanted to talk to the children and share the news with them.

Both Keyanna's and Kyara's children filled the house the next morning. They were having so much fun and it felt like a circus in the house. Hearing their voices awoke that joy of motherhood again in Keke's heart. She was getting ready to go out of her room and meet everyone. Of course, her children came to the room and hugged her when they got back from visiting their grandparents. She just hadn't seen the others yet. She slowly knelt down and said a prayer. She had been praying somewhat ever since the crash, but today she felt good about doing it again for a long time. She sang songs of worship a bit before saying her prayers.

"Father, forgive me. I haven't been myself lately. I have questioned you and wondered why you have been so silent. I know your words and I also know you have a great plan for me. However, right now I am finding it hard to accept that. I miss my husband and I really want to believe that he isn't dead. Maybe it's because a body hasn't been found or because a part of me still feels him alive. I don't know what to think or say anymore for my thoughts are all mixed up. My emotions are off the roof. I know you see it and all and I humbly ask for your help. Be my strength when I am weak. Be my light when I feel like I am in the dark and give me the patience and tools to be able to be there for my kids. I feel like I am about to start another chapter again and this time alone. Though I know I am never alone because I have you, I am lonely because I lost my partner. I pray wherever he is, he will find peace and will know that I will forever love him. I thank you for all of it and help me, Lord. Amen."

She finished the prayer and met with her family. She gathered her kids around her and talked to them as she would always.

"Sophie, Janis, and Elodie, you all know how much Mommy and Daddy love you. You also know that Daddy has been on a trip for a while. I know you miss him and I do, too. Today, I want to tell you something. Daddy is still on a trip."

"When is he coming back?" asked Elodie.

Keyanna tried hard to not cry. She responded, "He isn't coming back because he went to stay with God."

"You mean in heaven?" asked Sophie.

"Yes, he is in heaven with God. He won't come back but he is always in our hearts. Do you guys understand that?"

The children looked a bit confused but just ran to their mother and gave her a huge hug.

Beau stepped in and said to them, "You will feel sad from time to time because you can't see Daddy anymore. But remember how Grandpa talked to you guys about angels?"

They all nodded.

Beau continued, "Well, Daddy has earned his wings and he is now an angel watching over you guys. Mommy will still be here to do everything with you and we will also. But Daddy will visit you sometimes through dreams and always protect you from bad people."

Keyanna's parents stepped in and told them, "You, children, will still come to visit us and do anything fun that you want."

The children seemed to have understood everything that everyone shared. Keyanna couldn't tell much from her first two children's reactions because communication was still hard. She knew they would struggle because they loved their father. She would strive to make sure to fill that void as much as she could.

Once the kids went back to playing, she thanked everyone and asked them to give her some time to get back to herself, and then she would announce when preparations could start for Jules. They all agreed with her and were actually okay with hearing those words from her.

"Thank you for including us in this discussion with the children," said Beau.

Keyanna thanked him and then spoke to the group. "Of course, they are familiar with all of you and with this hard news, I wanted them to have all the familiar faces around them. I am glad it went well. I'm just not sure what the days ahead will be like. One thing I know is that the children have that resilience that I used to have, too, and they believe we will all overcome this."

Beau said, "Indeed, we will. I have to get going, Keke, call me if you need me. I hear Kyara will be staying to help you more and I am happy about that. I know she will take good care of you."

"Yes, I know she will and I am thankful for her also," replied Keyanna.

Beau went to kiss his grandkids and Kyara's children before leaving.

Soon after, Keke's parents left to do errands they had to do for the day.

Her mom reminded Keyanna that Eric was the one dropping off the meals today.

"That won't be necessary, Mom. I want to cook for my children today. I want to start doing those chores slowly. But I will need the contact of the cleaning lady so she can start again."

"I will send that over right away," Mother said.

That night, Keyanna made homemade pizza for the family. She felt a little more at ease in the kitchen again. She realized that she missed this experience. She loved cooking and she hadn't done that almost for three months now. Her mom's and best friend's meals were good, but it was a great feeling to find herself cooking again. She would continue to try and stop the meal delivery for now. She had taken a mental note also to send out thank you cards to everyone who had helped with it. They all enjoyed the meal and the kids helped clean up.

The dinner was followed by a great movie that both friends watched and a pleasant conversation about what Keyanna had missed while on her trip. Kyara filled her in about her small business and the clients. Keyanna also shared how she had thought of not going back to work.

Keyanna explained, "I think this experience is making me rethink my life and I want to work just for me. I don't think that I want to move forward with my current organization."

"You have time to think," Kyara reassured her, "so don't rush that decision yet. Either way, you will be fine. I think you have a great list of clientele to support you and the children financially."

"I will continue to pray about it and see where it leads me," Keyanna replied.

Thirty Five

The past week had been so hard for Eric. He really wanted to discuss his child with Keyanna. Though he knew that was a wrong idea, he couldn't help it. He hadn't seen her for over two weeks now. The meal delivery was an outlet for him to see her and to get a peek at his child, too. The idea of having a child and not knowing for almost ten years was disturbing to him. He had missed a lot in her life already and didn't want to miss anything more. Keyanna had asked for time with the family to get back to herself before the burial, but he was, for sure, going to talk to her after the funeral. Eric had visited his dad this past week to discuss the situation with him. He learned that his father was also aware of Sophie.

Eric was mad at his father but, then again, he couldn't blame him for he had acted really bad. That's not enough of a reason for letting him be a fool and staying in the dark for so long. He had learned that Sophie wasn't aware of Eric being her father either. The only father she ever knew and, maybe would always know, was Jules. He didn't want to upset her world, but he just wanted to hear from Keyanna and know how he could be a part of her life. He would really love that. Hopefully, this would be something that Keke would be open to.

Nicole had placed a call to Keyanna today to check on her. They had developed a great friendship over time. They checked on each other and supported each other. Nicole knew the stages of grief and had her own share of loss. So she promised to be there for Keyanna and to give her the moral support that she needed. Nicole noticed that Keyanna was getting better this last week. She had shared with Nicole that she had started therapy and had spent a lot of time journaling. Some days were hard but she was finding the strength to live again. The greatest reason for this was her children.

Nicole understood that completely. Ever since Grace had joined the family as a new member, she had found another reason to be her best and give everything she had to her kids. She loved them with everything she had in her. Brice was over the moon with having a sister. He found himself singing to her all the time. He was even playing big brother on some duties that his mom had assigned to him. She just loved the love she saw in Brice's eyes every time he looked at Grace. Even her mother had found some type of new hope. Surely, Grace had brought joy and blessings her way.

Once their call ended, Keyanna joined her friend at the pool where the kids were having a blast. The weather was getting warmer each day and she was happy. She loved summer, though many would not agree because of the humidity that it brought to the plains. It had been almost two months since she started getting back to her "old" self from cooking for her family, doing laundry, and just doing the normal routine things. She had been gaining back her energy slowly and surely. There were days when she still struggled but somehow she found her way back to reading the Bible for comfort, talking to her best friend, journaling, and also going to therapy. Having her friend in the house was helping also with the loneliness. She was so thankful for Kyara that words couldn't express it. She thanked God every day for her.

Deep down, she was slowly accepting the fact that her husband would not come back, but she was also not in a rush to dismiss the thought that he might. The last she heard from Caleb, the cleaning crew was rounding up with cleaning the island. There was still work to be done but still no sign of Jules. She just didn't understand how someone could just disappear like that from a crash. Whatever this was, one day there would be an answer for it. She looked back at her family and didn't want to miss any more time spent with them. She wanted to be present. Her children had missed that this past month and she wanted to give it all back. She knew what it meant to be in the household but not truly be there. She had always vowed not to be that type of parent because her mother used to be the queen of that.

Beau had been struggling these past weeks. He wanted to bury his son and move on to mourn him. Though there wasn't a body, he still wanted to have a service for him and remember him for all that he was and more. He loved his son and it would be a deep pain for him to be the one to bury him, but he wanted to. It seemed like heaven had decided that he would be the only person left out of his family. He missed his wife and now his son which made it hard at times. He had been trying to find comfort in God's Word, but he was human. Sometimes, it didn't work. Kyara had suggested that he talk to someone but he didn't see the reason why he should. He was just praying that Keyanna would come around and agree to have a service for his son.

Beau had talked with his brother and some distant family members and they all planned to come to the service and be there to support him. He had even thought about the place and some type of arrangement that could be done for Jules. He also heard that the airline had a service for all the victims and also had put flowers and bouquets around the entire island to remember them. Though there was still a tiny hope that his son's body might be found given the cleaning crew was still there, he had refused to put his focus on that.

Thirty Six

Caleb woke up from his dream sweating and wondering when this whole thing would stop. He didn't know if it was his mind messing with him or his real feelings. These past weeks, his dreams had gotten stronger. He saw Nicole everywhere and just couldn't reach her in his dreams. He had realized that he had fallen for her the first day he saw her, but how could he tell this to Nicole was the question. He had called her many times but didn't have the courage to tell her. He didn't know how to go about it. He could easily hear his father's voice reminding him to just be himself in matters like this.

But how can I? he kept asking himself. *This is Nicole.* She was a lady he had learned who was independent and strong-willed. She didn't let anything stop her and she believed the right man would come for her. *What if she didn't see me as the right man? Or what if I'm not good enough?* He checked the time and it was still late in the night. He decided to get some water and try to go back to sleep.

Caleb eventually fell back asleep and woke up later by a phone call. Though he was partially still asleep, he recognized the number and picked up the phone. It was Keyanna. She called to see if there was any news from the cleaning team. He was devastated to tell her but he had to.

"No, Keyanna, we haven't found any more bodies, and the crew's last day on the island is later today. They will wrap up the operation and head back to our headquarters."

Keyanna stayed mute for a long while and then thanked Caleb for the information.

Caleb told her, "I will inform you if anything else comes up." Then he hung up.

This is the news that she needed to share with everyone. But right now, she just wanted to focus on healing and getting better. She had been enjoying these past few days with her children. She knew healing wouldn't be complete if she didn't give a befitting burial for her husband. She found it hard given there wasn't a body. Right now, she was getting ready for a therapy session and also had to go follow up with her doctor. Her day was filled. The children also had swimming lessons later on that day. Ever since they shared the news about their father with the kids, things hadn't been the same.

Sophie who was so close to her father, would wake up many times throughout the night asking for him. She would then go over a rehearsed story she created about how angels watched over everyone and her father was doing that even though he wasn't with them in person. Keyanna's heart broke each time this happened but, deep down, she knew this would continue for a long time before the kids fully understood. She didn't even know if they would truly understand but she prayed for them and herself every day. Somehow, she had found her way back to the scriptures and to God. As she always said, "If God saw me through my pregnancy with Sophie, He will see me through everything."

The next day, Keyanna had informed the family that she was ready to organize her husband's burial. She had no idea how things worked but Kyara had gathered information on some companies in town that could assist them with the process. So her family and Kyara planned it, but they still asked for her input for flower arrangements and how the service hall should be set up. The service was confirmed for the following week on Saturday. Caleb and Nicole had promised to come and so did one agent from the airline.

To be honest, she was impressed with the airline company. They really did care about everything. She recalled how easy the process was to get the funds for the loss of Jules's life when she was working with them. During those times, she was just going with the flow. Her spirit wasn't around here at all. She was still stuck at the beach with the high hope of finding her husband. She checked out physically and spiritually for real. She was thankful that she was coming back to her former self because her children and family wouldn't be able to go on like that. According to her physician, as of yesterday, she didn't need the sleeping pills anymore.

Keyanna slowly had found herself sleeping and eating normally. Heck, she was even cooking meals for her family. She admitted that she missed Jules goofing around the kitchen when she was cooking. Truly, she would forever miss her husband. She might slowly accept the reality, but it didn't mean it would be pain-free. Her nights were still longer than her days. She usually found herself sleeping more often on the carpet than in her own bed. At times, she coped with wearing his clothes just to smell his cologne; it felt like home next to her. She prayed it would get better, but Jules was the love of her life and her soulmate and she had no idea how that pain would ever ease.

She tried to stay focused one day at a time and trusted that heaven would give her strength and all that she needed to continue. Keyanna had made majors changes these past two months. She had finally let go of her full-time job and planned to return to her business fully in a month or so. Right now, Kyara still covered for her on that job and heaven couldn't bless this sister enough. Keyanna didn't know what she did to deserve a wonderful person like Kyara as a friend and sister, but she was thankful and didn't take her for granted. She was planning to surprise Kyara and Alfred with a vacation for a week in the Bahamas after the funeral as a thank you gift for all they had done these past months for her and her children. She had also planned on giving a weekend getaway to Branson to her parents. As for Eric, he would get a thank you card.

Talking about Eric, she knew she had to clear up things with him one of these days; she just wasn't ready for that right now. She wanted to bury her husband, get back to their own routine, and someday, she would take care of that particular headache. A knock at the door brought her attention back to the person standing in front of it.

"Hi, you," Janis said to his mother.

Janis was the quietest of her three children. He was very sensitive and could feel so much.

"Come here," she said.

He ran to his mom and gave her the best hug ever.

"Do you need something, big boy?" she asked.

"I want a snack," he said.

"Okay, let's go find you a snack," Keyanna suggested.

Janis was tall for his age and had a huge appetite. His dad would always tease him by calling him his mini-giant. Surely, he would take after his father. He favored him a lot and, hopefully, he would play basketball as Jules did. Keyanna found herself dazing again and wondered about all the things Jules was going to miss out on if he was truly dead.

Dead? Yes, she had finally accepted that word. It wasn't easy though because she had it in her mind that her husband never really said goodbye so he would be still alive somehow. It was during a session in therapy that she had to recall a scene where she realized that they did say goodbye. When the plane was going through turbulence, she remembered praying with him. He told her how much he loved her and was thankful for her. He even said to her to take care of herself and the children in case they didn't make it or if he didn't make it. Her brain had suppressed that memory until she was introduced to MDR, a form of trauma therapy. It had been helping her a lot and, today, she had accepted the fact that her husband was no more.

She came back to herself and gave snacks to Janis and his siblings. She had been experiencing these moments a lot and forgetting about herself in a situation or thought. Everyone said it was normal and that she had gone through a lot these past weeks and should give herself some grace.

"You will get better and find yourself," they all had said.

She sure hoped so.

Thirty Seven

The hall was well decorated with flowers just like she had planned. It looked lovely, something she believed that Jules would have loved, not that they had ever talked about their funeral and what it would look like. They didn't even have a will written because they believed they still had time to write one up. After all, they were just in their thirties. *Who dies in their thirties? Well, I guess Jules. He was called home too soon.* She glanced around and took time to check every detail of the hall. The service was going to be led by Keyanna's father given his position in the church. She didn't mind because she knew he was a good man and great father, except for the time when he didn't stand up for her against her mother. All that was in the past now, and together with her family and Jules's family, they were here to pay their last tributes to Jules.

She made sure their children were also present along with Nicole and her family, Caleb, his mother, Eric, and some of Jules's family and friends as well. Alfred spoke after the service of how wonderful his best friend was and how he missed him dearly. Keyanna didn't want to speak at first when planning was going on but today she did so with her children holding her hands.

"I have loved my husband and I miss him so much. I also know that he deserves peace wherever he is and this I pray will give him that peace. I thank every one of you for coming and I ask that you keep us in your prayers," she said.

Once the service was over, they all gathered in the next hall where they celebrated Jules's life because Keyanna didn't want everyone to feel so sad around her and the children. So they enjoyed wonderful dishes of food that Jules loved and they all paid their respects individually by saying a word or two to Keyanna and Jules's family. Finally, they buried an empty casket in memory of him and filled it with his favorite items: his guitar, saxophone, and a few of his favorite pairs of sneakers.

Keyanna wanted it that way; it gave her some type of mental relief. His tombstone would be ready in a few weeks. She looked around in the hall and saw the familiar faces and others that weren't familiar. She thanked God for He had given her the strength that she had asked for these past months.

Standing next to the casket, thinking through it all, how Jules's infidelity led them to the retreat, and now this, she recalled that faithful prayer: "Let your will be done" was what she said when she had found out he was cheating and thought that their union couldn't survive. They did and shared the most amazing (and never experienced before) week of their lives together. She then recalled how her dad used to tell her, "When we ask God for His will to be done in our lives, it doesn't always align with our will. We ought to be ready that His will sometimes will lead us into unknown destinations."

The END

Epilogue

Heading into the restaurant, Keyanna wondered why she ever agreed to meet him here. She knew this was bound to happen but she surely wasn't ready for it. She had dodged him for almost six months now with the same excuses. She was healing, back to revamping her business, and too tired after caring for the children. She truly didn't have much time to sit down and talk with anyone except her best friend and parents. But when Eric's calls continued, she knew it was time to meet him.

She quickly spotted him at a table and headed toward him. Greetings were exchanged and she settled down in a chair.

"Thanks for meeting with me today. I know you are busy and I completely understand so I am grateful," Eric said.

"You're welcome. Though I have a feeling why you want to meet, I will let you speak first," Keyanna began.

Eric asked her, "Do you want anything to drink first?"

"Sure, a club soda will do."

Eric gave a wave to the server who brought Keyanna's drink to her.

"Once again, thank you," said Eric. "I wanted to meet because I wanted a better understanding of what you told me months back on the last day I had delivered meals to you and the children."

"Yes, so now I know why you called me then. I knew this topic would resurface knowing you. I wasn't ready to talk about it," Keyanna admitted.

"I'm sorry but I want to know more about the pregnancy and Sophie."

"Well," began Keyanna, "you and I have never had a decent conversation about us since that faithful day. First of all, there is no "us" anymore. And secondly, Sophie is your biological daughter. She is but she doesn't need to know that because her real father is in heaven now watching over her as an angel."

Eric swallowed his water hard and then spoke, "I know that I am in no position to demand anything from you right now but she does need to know her biological father and I want to be part of her life."

Keyanna looked straight at Eric. "I don't think so. So you actually called me for that?" asked Keyanna. "Yes, you deserve to know that she is yours and I just told you but you don't get to choose who her father should be at this point. Where were you when she was been born into this world? Did you even know you had impregnated me? How dare you, Eric. Now all of a sudden, you think you have the right to be part of her life. I admit, it was foolish of me to have kept this from you all this while but at least your parents knew about her. So I haven't really wronged you. Now, if you will excuse me, I have better things to do than sit here and watch you tell me all this craziness."

Keyanna grabbed her things and walked out on Eric.

To be continued...

Acknowledgements

To my heavenly father who loves me beyond measure and who took the time to make me so beautifully and wonderfully. I am nothing without Yahweh. The gift, the talent, creativity and all are blessings from Him and I am thankful.

To my earthly father, words will fail me as usual but know that I am so grateful to have a dad like you. You have never stop believing in me and praying for me. Your zeal for me to be my best version and get the best in life is appreciated. I hope I will continue to make you proud; for you gave that little child a chance to dream…… and I am beyond thankful. Love you!

To my mother, you saw my gift of writing before I did. Your encouragement and your hope to see me excel beyond what the world has set for me is seen and so much appreciated. Love you and thank you for all the sacrifices you made for me to exist and thrive.

To my husband, my king! I thank you for always putting up with my stubborn self in the most gracious way. Your love, support and care doesn't go unnoticed. I am thankful and grateful to heaven for you.

To my grandmother Lucie, who loved me more than life itself. I miss you and I hope you stay forever proud. I hope you get to see from above the wonderful impact your teaching of God has made on my life and now your great grandchildren live as well.

Of course, all of this wouldn't have been done without my community and those that are dear to my heart. There are so many of you ladies, I can't begin to write all the names here, but I do want to say thank you to the few below.

D.M. Whitaker, Jamalia Parker, Andrea Foster, Tiffani Holmes, Saji Johnson, Tameshia Harris, Chaima Dan-Merogo, Martine Quartey, Nikki Taylor, Andree Seri-Viho, Irene Gbaguidi, Tomegee Seri, Lovely Taylor, Adjele Amegnizin, Aesha Mitchell, Debra Paris, Shade Adeleke, Vickie Stone, Adjo Goke, Stacey McClain-Hunnicutt, Lynda Tsogbe.

You all have made an impact or two in this journey I called life and I am grateful. More Grace and Blessings are my prayers for you all....

About the Author

Sarah Videgla is originally from Togo, a small country in the western side of Africa. There she gained a great love and an amazing creativity from stories her grandparents would usually tell her around the moonlight fire and more. Those stories awaken the passion of writing in her; hence propelling her to write stories that will heal, give hope, and remind others that God has the last say and to never give up. Sarah loves to write novels and short stories, and also children's books. She also has this creative side which enables her to create products beyond her books for her customers through both her online and brick and mortar store.

Sarah currently lives in Omaha, NE with her husband and three amazing kids. She enjoys being a wife, a mother, an author, a business consultant and mentor, and an entrepreneur. When she is not busy with her daily activities, you can find her nurturing her children of which two are autistic and giving back to the community as much as she can.

Stay connected with Sarah Videgla and get bundles, freebies and more at sarahvidegla.com

Follow her on Facebook: @ **Author Sarah Videgla**

DOWLOAD A FREEBIE:

CHECK OUT MORE FROM AUTHOR:

Notes

1. Dr Temple Grandin "The Autistic Brain": https://www.templegrandin.com
2. Togo (West Africa) https://en.wikipedia.org/wiki/Togo
3. Boston Island: https://www.bostonharborislands.org
4. Igbo People: https://www.britannica.com/topic/Igbo
5. Ewe People: https://en.wikipedia.org/wiki/Ewe_people
6. City of Lille, France: https://en.wikipedia.org/wiki/Lille
7. City of Paris, France, Eiffel Tower: https://www.toureiffel.paris/en/the monument/history
8. Le Tagine Restaurant, France: http://letagine.fr
9. Val D'Europe: https://val-d-europe-en.klepierre.fr
10. City of Brussels: https://www.brussels.be
11. Dr Terrerai "Awakened Woman" https://tererai.org/index.php/product/awakened-book
12. Lost Kitchen: https://www.findthelostkitchen.com